1

Behind the Smile

A Love Eternal

Joseph W. Bebo

J.W.M. Bebo Books

Joseph W. Bebo
Hudson, MA, 01749
Email: joewbebobooks@gmail.com
Editor: James Oliveri

Test Readers: Kathy Bebo, Chris Ransier
Proof Reader: Paul Kelloway

Library of Congress Cataloging in – Publication Data
Joseph W. Bebo
Behind the Smile – A Love Eternal /Joseph Bebo – First Edition

ISBN: 979-8-9864044-1-7
Romance, Historical

This book is dedicated to my wife, Kathleen, whose smile won my heart

Chapter 1 – The Duomo

The republic of Florence in 1492 was a wonderful place to be. At carnival, when the streets were dressed with colorful banners and the people were costumed and masked for the balls, it was a dazzling thing to see, especially if you were a thirteen-year-old girl. Anytime you were on your own was a special day, but during carnival it was an adventure.

Not actually alone, for that would be odd indeed, but to be about with your brothers and sisters, with no adult in sight, at least none who could tell you what to do. That was almost as good. Lisa could hardly catch her breath as they dashed about here and there, bright-eyed and breathless.

"Where do we go next?" asked Nolto, her youngest brother, the smallest of four.

"We are going to the Duomo, the most beautiful cathedral in all of Italy," said Giovangual, the older of her male siblings. "I am meeting Giuliano there. He is a Medici."

"Big deal," replied Nolto. "I want to go to the zoo. They have a wild panther there."

"Your sister can take you," answered his older brother.

"I want to go to the Duomo with you," said Lisa. "Ginevera can take them to the zoo."

"No, one of us has to go with them," said Giovangual. "They are too young to go alone, not here in the city after dark."

"It is not dark yet," Lisa replied. "Do you not want to see the great Duomo, Nolto? It is the largest dome in the world. Is that not right, Giovangual?"

Giovangual did not answer. He did not want his brothers and sisters tagging along when he met the Medici boy. He especially didn't want his older sister, Lisa, there hogging the conversation.

"Si, I guess so," said Nolto. "But the wild panther is from some place far away. It is fierce and we may never see it again, as it travels around the world."

"Then it is settled. Giovangual will take you," announced Lisa.

"No, I will not," he objected. "I cannot. It is out of the question."

"I am the oldest," Lisa reminded him. "You will do as I say or you will all go home."

"You cannot order us about," responded Giovangual, who was getting tired of his older sister bossing him around. She was always telling him what to do, a big know-it-all, who acted as if she was ten years older rather than just a year and a half.

"Oh yes I can," replied his older sister. "Remember what father said."

"He said to stay together," her sister Ginevera informed them.

"Then we can all go to the Duomo with Giovangual," Lisa stated.

"That won't do. I have to meet Giuliano," said her brother.

"Go with them to the zoo then," insisted Lisa. "I will go and meet Giuliano. I knew him before you did. We have the same birthday. I have as much right to meet him again as you - more. Take them to the zoo. I will bring our friend. And don't you dare go home without me. I will meet you here."

Before her younger brother could object, she was rushing across the crowded street toward the large domed church in the center of the walled city.

As she walked through the crowd the excitement affected her like a bolt of lightning. Her nerves tingled. Her blood rushed. Her breath grew faster. She felt like she would explode. She was free, free for the first time in her life. It was both exhilarating and frightening, as if she were out on a high wire over the steeples.

She wondered if Giuliano would remember her. After all, it had been almost seven years. They were only children when they were together for a short time during a carnival like this, for Florence had them every year. She was sure she would recognize him, with his beautiful head of black curls and his broad, straight shoulders.

She had seen him a few times since, though only from a distance at family gatherings or on the streets. Every time she did, her heart skipped a beat. It had been a couple of years. She wondered what he looked like now. He would be easy to spot, for she knew where he would be waiting. He was expecting her brother, not her. He would not recognize her in any case. She had a mask on.

She resolved to play a trick on him and not reveal her identity. Perhaps she could beguile him with her charm and wit and capture his heart. It was worth a try. It would be fun, and besides, she wanted to meet a handsome prince and live happily ever after, like the maidens in the new novels that were just now being printed. Giuliano fit the bill.

At thirteen, she was the oldest in her family, the daughter of a landowner. Although of noble blood, they were from a minor branch of the family and poor, as her father continually told them. She would have to be married off if they were to prosper again. What better than to be wed to a wealthy banker's son, a young attractive one to boot.

Her friend Elizabeth was only thirteen and she was the head of a household, with servants and cooks under her command. She had married well. She had special meals prepared for her, rich clothes, and a sumptuous bed that she shared with her husband. He was only a few years older than her and not some senile old man.

If she was not careful, she might end up with an old farmer. No, better she wed a rich, gorgeous boy like Giuliano.

As she approached the plaza, she began to search for him. Her heart beat fast with anticipation.

Chapter 2 – The Charade

She spotted him in the Piazza, next to a side door to the cathedral. He wore a short tunic of gold and gray brocaded silk, with gray stockings and black, shiny shoes. His hair was long and curly, his eyes dark and penetrating. He was more handsome now than he had been as a child. His broad shoulders and strong legs made her pupils dilate.

She approached him brazenly.

"Are you waiting for someone, dear sir?" she said.

The youth looked up in surprise, shocked to be addressed so by a lone girl.

"Why yes, although it is no concern of yours," Giuliano replied.

"Ah, but it is. I have come in your friend's stead."

"Who are you, dear lady," he inquired.

"I am the person you are to meet."

"I have come to see Antonmaria di Noldo's son, Giovangual."

"Giovangual has been detained and sent me to apologize. Perhaps I might keep you company in his place."

"Why are you masked?"

"It is carnival. Everyone is masked but you, dear sir."

"I will mask for the ball," he answered. "For now I am just myself waiting for a friend. So, tell me please, to whom do I have the pleasure of speaking?"

"It would not be proper to reveal myself so soon. I hardly know you, Signore. Perhaps at the ball."

"Oh, are you going?" he asked.

"If you take me, kind sir."

"Call me Giuliano. What shall I call you?"

"You can call me madam."

"Madam? That is not a name."

"It is a proper enough name for carnival, or you can call me Lucrezia's first born if you prefer."

"Ah, you are full of riddles," he said. "Are you as good a dancer as you are a jokester?"

"I am told I am a good dancer, and I make no jokes, sir. I only want someone to take me to the ball. If you cannot oblige me, then …"

"Oh, but I will oblige you, dear miss. For you are the first interesting person I have met all night. I will learn your name."

"If you must, but is not the mystery worth not knowing? Live in suspense, I say, not knowing what the next moment brings. What better way to spend carnival than dancing under the stars with a stranger."

"All right, Madam it is. Will you accompany me to the ball?" he asked.

"I would be delighted, dear sir," she replied.

"And you will tell me your name," he assured her.

"Perhaps," she answered, "that and much more."

The music of the orchestra, brought all the way from Milan, could be heard through the open windows of the ballroom of the Pallazzo della Signoria. The room, large enough to accommodate 200 people, was full to capacity with the cream of the city's society.

They entered the room through two large, ornate doors and were shocked to find it completely dark inside. The only light came from countless tiny candles on the ceiling, thousands of them. It was as if instead of being in a room, they were walking under a clear night sky full of numberless shining stars.

"How amazing." Lisa said. "It is like we are outside. There are thousands of lights. I have never seen such a thing."

The combination of starry lights and rapturous music was dazzling. Lisa felt like she had drunk champagne, though nothing had passed her lips since supper.

"Ah, it is the Master," Giuliano said. "My father told me he was coming. He is with the orchestra from Milan, where he now lives, although he is from these parts. He did the same thing for his patron, the Duke of Milan. My father, Lorenzo, sent him as a gift from our city. Now they have stolen him. He will not come back. He is here for the carnival, however. He has a number of other wondrous inventions if you would like to see the pageant tomorrow."

"I would rather dance with you tonight, my lord," Lisa replied.

"You speak so dramatically. Are you an actress? Is that who you are?"

"Perhaps if you dance with me you will learn," she told him.

The band was playing a slow, stately Spanish song, with a triple meter. There was something naughty about it, a sensuous undercurrent. It made Lisa's blood warm and made her want to move her limbs.

They were soon on the dance floor together, a huge space covered with couples. All were dressed in costumes of one sort or another. Giuliano had put on his mask, a white one with a black mustache. It covered most of his face. Lisa fit right in with her crimson cape and long flowing black gown. Her crimson mask only covered her eyes and nose. Her full lips and smile were visible to all.

When he grabbed her around the waist, she thought she would die. She held her breath until she almost passed out. Only when he let her go did she breathe again.

At some point - she hardly noticed when - a different song was playing, faster and gayer than the first. She found herself being swung around and around as if on a revolving swing. It was like she had just woken up from a deep sleep and didn't know how she got there. It didn't seem real. Finally, the music stopped and she fell into his arms.

For a moment the world had ceased to be and she was in a soundless web of happiness. She had never felt such joy. She was breathing hard. Her heart beat rapidly. She felt suspended in a dream, a mirage, where no other sight or sound could penetrate. The music, the surroundings, the boy-man with the strong arms and beautiful hands holding her, transported her to another place, a different world, some other universe.

Giuliano was also carried away with the enchantment of the moment. He was a fairly sophisticated youth. He would be ruler of the city one day like his father was now, and had been taught about things sexual. He had even slept in bed with a young lady his age, a prospective wife. Although the stocking suit that encased his arms and legs like a potato sack, and the chaperone, made things rather less than romantic. This, however, was something different. What was happening to him now had not happened to him before.

He had never held such an alluring object in his arms. He had never touched a body like this before, flesh so soft and voluptuous he wanted to eat it. Something was happening to him. It had happened before when he saw the maids bathing. It happened now when he held this strange girl. He wanted to hold her more, but the dance was over. The song had ended.

"I must go," she whispered as she rushed from the dance floor. "I will be late."

"Wait, don't go," he said, racing after her. "The night has just begun."

"No, I must be back," she answered. "I promised. Thank you for taking me to the ball."

"No, wait," he said. "I must see you again. I love you. Tell me your name."

"Call me Mona," she replied. "Meet me here tomorrow night."
With that, she was gone, a small smile playing on her lips.

Chapter 3 – Fatherly Advice

"Where have you been?" Lisa's brother, Giovangual, asked angrily. "We have been waiting forever."

"You exaggerate, brother," replied Lisa. "You could not have waited more than a short time."

"It does not matter. You said you would be here and you were not. You lied. I am telling papa."

"Go ahead, and I will tell him you were going to go off and leave us."

"You are the one that left, not I," he objected

"I went to meet your friend, so that he would not wait idly for you, since you were not coming. I did you a courtesy. You should thank me."

"Ah, you are always twisting things around. You make me miserable."

"Do not complain," she said. "Come, let us go or we will all be in trouble."

They arrived at their family's rented villa on via de Pepi, near Santa Croce, a short time later.

"You are late," their father, Antonmaria, said as soon as they entered. "You will not be allowed to go out unattended with the other children if you cannot return on time."

"It is all Lisa's fault," her brother, Giovangual, said. "She left us and did not come back when she promised. We had to wait a long time for her."

"That is not true," Lisa objected. "They did not wait but a short time. I was on an errand and got caught in the crowds."

"I do not want to hear excuses," insisted her father. "You are not to be about alone. I want you home when you say. You must stay with your brothers and sisters or you will not go out again. Do I make myself clear?"

"Yes, Papa. I am sorry. It will not happen again," Lisa promised.

Later that evening, when alone with her father, Lisa told him what had really occurred.

"I met a boy," she said, breathlessly. "His name is Giuliano. He is the son of the great Lorenzo de Medici."

"What? You are meeting boys unattended? Do you want to get a bad reputation? No one in good standing will want you after that. Are you trying to ruin our prospects? We are counting on you to make a good marriage."

"I was masked," she responded. "No one could recognize me, nor could the boy. He took me to the ball and danced with me. He told me he loved me."

"A Medici, you say? Giuliano?"

"Si, Papa. I met him when I was eight."

"Si, I know the boy. He is Lorenzo's third born. Your stepmother is his cousin. He will be ruler of Florence one day. You are setting your sights rather high, my daughter."

"Did you not tell us to aim high and we might hit our target. Better to overshoot your goal than to come up short."

"I believe he is promised to another."

"He is in love with me."

"Be careful, my dear," her father advised. "You are not to meet him un-chaperoned. A boy may say he loves you when it is not so just to have you in bed. Then when you are with child he will throw you over for another. There are many unwed mothers who have been treated so. Be careful you do not become another."

"It is not like that, Father," she replied. "I know what I am doing."

"That may be, but I do not want you alone with him without proper attendance. Invite him here if you want, but do not see him alone or you will not go out at all."

"But, Father, I …"

"No buts, Lisa. Do as I say or you will be an old crone before you leave this house unattended again."

"Yes, Father, I am sorry. Whatever you say."

That night Lisa did not sleep. It wasn't the light snoring of her three sisters that kept her up. It was the rapid beating of her heart as she relived that evening at the ball. The thrill of it made her want to dance across the room, twirling around and around like she had in her lover's arms.

A few miles away at the Medici villa, Giuliano was experiencing much the same thoughts. The young woman in the crimson cloak and mask haunted his dreams. He had never been so captivated by another. Her skin looked so smooth, her mouth so succulent. Her hair was like silk. Her image bewitched his mind. Who was she? Where did she come from? Would he ever see her again, or was she just a figment of his imagination? He could hardly wait for the morrow, his mind consumed with what might come to be.

Chapter 4 – Motherly Advice

The next day, Lisa went through her chores mindlessly, in anticipation of her evening rendezvous. She had never done anything like this before, but desperate times called for desperate measures. If she was to be married to save the family from a bleak future, she would have a say in the matter.

Why not set her sights high? She had just as much right as the next girl to a good marriage. She imagined herself the head of a rich household, ordering servants and merchants around, men and women twice her age. She would be kind like her mamma was with the menial classes but demand the respect her station was due. She and Giuliano would make a good team as husband and wife.

But she was getting ahead of herself. She had captivated him. She had yet to win him. That she would do tonight.

They had not taught her much, her papa and mamma, although they had been quick to lecture her on her duty to the family. As the first-born daughter to a frayed minor branch of a noble family that duty was clear – marry a wealthy and kind man.

It had been drilled into her from a young age. She was thinking these thoughts when her stepmother interrupted her.

"Lisa."

"Si, Mamma."

"I understand you met a boy."

"Si, Mamma."

"This boy, he likes you?"

"Si, Mamma."

"Do I know this boy? Is he my cousin, Giuliano?"

"Si, Mamma."

"That is good. He is a nice boy. He will rule Florence one day soon if things go well. He is not promised yet, but things are so uncertain with the French and Rome. They change from day to day. Are you planning on seeing this boy again?"

"He has asked me to meet him this night near the Piazza. There are street plays and pageants. It is so exciting with all the people and spectacles."

"We will have Maria go with you to chaperone. One must be careful to not be swept away with it all," her stepmother admonished her. "One must keep their head and not forget their purpose. You must always remember why you are there. Giuliano is a young boy, and young boys all think alike. He is interested in one thing and one thing alone – to take your chastity, and your chastity is your most important possession. It keeps you from destitution and destruction. Without it, you are nothing.

"You must entice him without surrendering yourself to him. Lure him to you without letting him assume too much.

"How do I do that?" asked Lisa, hardly believing it was her stepmother who was talking to her like this.

"Let him get to know you. Let him hold your hand. Touch his arms. See if they are hard or soft. Let him touch yours but nothing more. Look into his eyes. Are they clear? Do they look at you with ardor? Let him smell your hair. Maria will be there to make sure he does not get too forward or you too permissive. You must listen to her."

"But what if she is not there?" Lisa asked.

"You must never be without your chaperone, never!" said her stepmother forcefully. "Leave him at once. You should never be alone with a boy. Leave immediately if Maria is not with you."

"But he is not a monster. You are being hysterical," Lisa replied.

"If you value your chastity, you will do as I say. I will have no more discussion about it. You want to entice him, get him to fall in love with you, but do not let him treat you as an object to do with as he likes. You want him to say, 'When can I see you again' and treat you with chivalrous respect.

"Remember, you will have to infatuate him with your mind as well as your looks. You are a beautiful, alluring young girl, but he will be an important man and needs an intelligent, polished, and chaste woman by his side, a good mother as well as a friend. Show him that you can be that woman.

"Do you have anything you want to ask me, dear?" her stepmother asked finally.

"This is all too much, Mamma," said Lisa in exasperation. "I only wanted to meet him and walk the streets with him at carnival. I do not get out very much. If I am to marry, I want to marry someone my own age, someone I want, someone I can be in love with. I have loved Giuliano since I first saw him those seven years ago."

"Then do as I tell you, my child. Let your feelings guide you but always remember why you are there and what you must, in all cases, protect. If you do this, you will be fine. Stay to the twelfth hour, make him ask when he can see you again, and then depart."

A short time later, after the little ones were in bed, Lisa left for her rendezvous with Giuliano. She was excited, but also a little confused by all that her parents had told her. She would have liked it better if they did not know about it. Now instead of freedom, she felt pressured from the weight of her duty to the family.

The family servant, Maria, went with her, Lisa's mother being too busy watching her other children to chaperone her daughter. Her father, Antonmaria, as with most Italian men, was too proud. Maria had come with his first wife and had been with the family ever since. She was not happy to be watching her employers' daughter, but looked forward to getting out of the house during carnival.

Chapter 5 – The Rendezvous

Lisa thought she would be climbing out a rear window surreptitiously to rendezvous with her new beau. Now she found herself walking out the front door with her mother's and father's blessing. The meeting meant more to them, in a way, than it did Lisa. To her, being out with a boy was an exciting, daring adventure. To her parents it meant the survival of their impoverished family.

Lisa wore a long black cloak and her crimson mask. The first thing on the agenda was ditching her chaperone. Maria was heavy and middle-aged. She did not like to move fast, even when carrying out her household duties. The streets of the city were just as crowded as the night before. Everyone was costumed. Lisa walked as fast as she could into the middle of the crowded Piazza and disappeared in the sea of bodies.

Quickly losing Maria, she dashed through the throng of people, then circled back toward the Duomo, making sure her watchdog was nowhere in sight. Maria had made no attempt to keep up with her charge, but wandered around until she found a vendor selling pork sausages. She then settled down on a street-side bench with a flagon of wine and enjoyed the spectacle that was carnival.

Lisa headed for the side entrance of the Duomo, where she had met Giuliano the night before. There was no one there. She stood, looking left and right. Had she missed him? People rushed past her, but none of them was her paramour. After several minutes, when no one showed up, she started to search the Piazza. She had not taken three steps when someone spoke behind her.

"So you are still wearing your mask."

"It is still carnival," she replied, turning around and greeting Giuliano with a radiant smile. "Would you have me unmasked so soon?"

"Alas, I did not wear one. I prefer to appear as normal."

"And so one as comely as you should," she said boldly.

"One as pretty as you should do the same," he answered. "I would give anything to see your face."

"You shall, kind sir, but not here. There are too many people about."

They started to walk slowly around the Piazza del Duomo. Remembering what her mother had told her, she took his hand. The thrill of touching him consumed her. It was as if she moved on air. She could not think. She could not remember. She almost could not breathe, or rather she forgot to breathe, so caught up was she in the feeling of his beautiful hand. She wanted to touch more of him. Her body was awakening to something she did not know. He talked to her as they walked.

"I thought about you all day," he began. "I wondered who you might be and where you were from. It is not fair you do not tell me. I will not sleep until I know who you are."

"Then you may lose much sleep before you know me."

"Have no fear," he answered. "I plan to keep my eyes opened wide, so I can see you more fully. You are beautiful."

There were people everywhere. Many dressed in costumes and masks. Everyone was gay and lively. Singing could be heard close by. Lisa and Giuliano walked with their heads close together. He bent slightly to keep his mouth close to her ear so she could hear him.

They reached the corner of the Piazza and entered a pillared portico. Called the Loggia della Signoria, it was quiet with few people about. Going underneath an arch, they descended a broad staircase. Only a few lanterns lit the way.

They found themselves alone beneath a wide archway with thick walls and ceiling. A bench sat next to the wall. It was dark and secluded. They were alone. Not a sound penetrated the sheltered room.

"Do you love me?" she asked.

"Yes, I love you dearly," he replied.

"But you hardly know me," she said.

"That is why I want to know you better," he answered. "What is your name, Signora?"

Rather than wait for an answer, he put his hands on her lower ribs and pushed her back into the archway, kissing her on the lips. She froze. She felt totally possessed by him. His mouth seemed to hunger for her. He did not let go of her. She had never been kissed before, let alone like a wild beast. She forgot all about what her mother had told her.

The boy was likewise possessed. Who was this unknown girl? She yielded so deliciously it thrilled him. Her lips were so soft and luscious he felt he was melting into them. She was innocent, yet there was a hunger in her that promised more.

The top of her breast peaked over her chemise. It looked so delicious he exploded just seeing it. It was like nothing he had felt before, as if he had died but still his heart beat. It felt like he had wet himself but he had never felt such pleasure. Perhaps something had happened to him, like a stroke, and he would drop dead in a moment. In a way, he didn't care. He could think of no better way to die than in the arms of this beautiful girl.

Lisa noticed something changing in her lover as he kissed her again harder. It was like he was turning to stone. Had she enchanted him somehow? She held his shoulders. They felt so strong. She could feel the muscles contracting, the power in his body as it strained against her.

It was time to leave. She wondered if what happened would make her pregnant. She certainly went far beyond her mother's instructions.

"I must go," she said, hurriedly going up the steps and out of the Portico.

"Already? The night is still young," he objected following her. "I want to take you to see the pageant. My father will be taking part."

"No, I must go," she insisted.

"When can I see you again?" he asked.

"Here, the morrow next at the sixth hour," she answered, her heart beating faster than a Gypsy's tambourine as she hurried down the street with him after her.

Suddenly, she stopped and spun around as he ran up to her. Kissing him quickly on the lips, she turned and disappeared around the corner.

As luck would have it, she met Maria on the way home. Her chaperone was standing near the side entrance to the Duomo and feeling quite tipsy from too much wine. Together, they went the rest of the way, each promising not to tell on the other.

Chapter 6 – A Carriage Ride

This time when Lisa left him, Giuliano followed her. He was not about to lose her, not after this night of intimacy. He followed at a distance as she made her way from the center of town to the first district, near the southern part of the wall. There she entered a small, rather shabby villa in a noisy district of narrow streets, where butchers, tanners, wood carvers, and saddle makers, competed for attention with cobblers, blacksmiths, cloth merchants, and beggars.

It did not take him long to learn the villa was being rented to the Gherardini family. Giuliano recognized the name. Caterina di Mariotto Rucellai, Lisa's stepmother, was his cousin.

He smiled to himself when he remembered the little girl he spent a summer day with in the country, and the magical evening at carnival, when they marveled at the spectacle and promised to marry each other.

Lisa woke-up early the next morning and jumped out of bed. Rather, she did not so much wake as get up after lying awake most of the night. She had been too excited to sleep, recalling each moment together with her lover and imagining the next.

She hardly ate her breakfast, her stomach was such a bundle of nerves, and could barely stand still for a moment as she waited for the sixth hour to come. She was going on pure nervous energy, for she hadn't slept more than a few fitful hours. She was overwrought and tired, but happy nonetheless.

She did her chores listlessly, carelessly, and slowly, leaving the floors mostly un-swept and the dishes dirty.

"What is wrong with you today?" her stepmother complained. "Are you still day-dreaming of your rendezvous last night?"

"It was the most marvelous time," Lisa confessed. "I think Giuliano loves me."

"Si, but will he ask you to marry him? That is the question."

"He wants to see me again."

"Aye, that is a good start."

As Lisa was preparing to leave to meet Giuliano, under the pretext of going to the market, her sister, Ginevera, came running in.

"There is a carriage outside. It is come for you!" she yelled.

"It is Giuliano de Medici!" her stepmother said looking out the front window. "He has brought a carriage. Hurry, you must put on something more fitting. I have a gown that might fit you."

"I will see him as I am," Lisa replied. She had her hair braided and wore a pleated skirt, with a high neckline and full sleeves.

"There is no time. There is no time," Caterina repeated excitedly. "That will have to do. Hurry, Giuliano is waiting."

Lisa took her time and walked sedately to the front room of the house. Her mother followed closely behind, trying to make her step-daughter move faster. Exiting the villa to the courtyard they saw Giuliano standing in front of the carriage.

"Buongiorno Signorina," he said.

"Good day, kind sir," Lisa responded. "What is this? How did you find me?"

"I followed you home last night," he replied. "I thought you might want to go for a ride in the country."

"A ride in the country? And I thought you would want to be alone with me."

"I want the world to know of my love for you," he said.

"I think you proved that to me last night," she told him smiling.

"You won my love, dear miss, now do me the honor of riding with me. Your stepmother may join us if she likes."

"It would only be proper, dear sir," Lisa's stepmother agreed.

A few moments later, Lisa, Caterina, and the young Medici were being driven out of the city into the Florentine countryside. As they rode, Giuliano pointed out the sites.

The road meandered beside the Arno River, between lines of cypress trees. The Senese Clavey Hills rose in the near distance, their green sides crowded with villas, farms, vineyards, and orchards.

They stopped beside a broad field fringed with oak trees. A stone fence separated the road from the grass.

"This is a good place to stop and have lunch," Giuliano observed. "I have brought a basket. Unfortunately, I have only brought food for two."

"That is all right," said Lisa's stepmother. "You young ones go about and have fun. I will stay in the carriage with the driver and pass the day. Have a good time, but please stay in sight."

Lisa and Giuliano took the basket into the field and followed a path to the top of a knoll overlooking the meadow. There they spread out the blanket and sat down. They could see her stepmother sitting in the carriage below.

"At least she is in the shade," Lisa said.

"She will be comfortable and has a clear view of us," Giuliano replied.

"Then she should be happy," Lisa answered. "It was shrewd of you to follow me. I expected as much."

"Oh, how long did you think you could hide your identity from me? You like to play games, do you?"

"I would have been disappointed if you had not found me out, though I was not expecting the carriage."

"What were you expecting?"

"I did not know what to expect, though I longed to see you again."

"And I you. You are even more beautiful without the mask."

He was tempted to kiss her, but could not with her chaperone watching. Lisa's heart was pounding with anticipation. He took her hand and almost took her breath away.

"You have captivated me," he admitted. "Your name is Lisa. That is my cousin, Caterina, down there. I have known her since youth. I know your brother, Giovangual. I remember you."

"And I you. I have never forgotten that summer evening, even though we were just children."

"We are still children," he commented. "Though I feel like an old man sometimes."

"Have you come to take me away, kind sir?" she asked.

"Yes, I have come to take you away," he answered.

"To ask my father for my hand?" she said, not believing it might actually come to be.

He did not answer, but chewed a leg of chicken.

"That I cannot do until I talk to my father," he said after swallowing. "He does not know of our love, but I will tell him."

"When?"

"Tonight," he answered.

They spent the rest of the afternoon on the top of the knoll, looking out over the Tuscan landscape. They talked like kids again of all the things they were going to do, the children they would have and raise, the places they would go and see, the friends and relatives they would share along with their experiences. They daydreamed and fantasized. All the while, they stared at each other unabashedly, drinking in each other's visage.

She held his hands. They were beautiful – his long fingers, his well-manicured nails. His palms were smooth, with no calluses or rough spots, strong but with a soft touch.

She luxuriated in the cool texture of his skin, the feel of his knuckles and palm. The thought of his hands upon her, probing her, excited her to distraction. Without thought she raised his hand to her lips and kissed it.

"I will tell my father tonight," the young Medici said. "He has been busy lately with the French and the Sforzas and has not been feeling well, but he promised to talk to me. I will tell him I intend to ask Signore Gherardini, your father, for your hand."

"Oh, Giuliano," whispered Lisa passionately, bringing his hands to her lips again and keeping them there. "I love you so. This is wonderful. Like a dream come true."

She was crying now. Tears of happiness streamed from her bright brown eyes.

"Non piangere amore mio," he said tenderly, taking her hand and kissing it in turn. "Do not cry."

He wiped her cheek with a thumb, then dabbed her eyes with his handkerchief. She took it embarrassingly and continued.

"I am sorry," she said. "I did not get much sleep last night, thinking of you. This is all so unexpected."

"It is quite all right, my sweetheart. You are so beautiful. I will be yours forever."

Time seemed to stand still. Giuliano lay with his head resting on Lisa's lap telling her his dreams, while she twirled his dark curls with her fingers.

"I will be ruler someday," he told her. "I will make Florence the most beautiful city in Italy, the world. Father is too interested in sport and the joust. I will make Florence a city of peace, a city of art and love."

"It is already the most beautiful city in the world," observed Lisa.

"I will make it more beautiful, and you will be my queen."

"I will be your queen," she echoed, imagining what it would be like, even though Florence was a Republic and had no king or queen. In spite of this, the Medici lived like monarchs in rich villas and palaces.

"What will it be like when we are married?" she asked.

"I will make you get up early in the morning and scrub the villa floors, then cook breakfast for me. Then I will make you carry the water and firewood upstairs."

"I can do that at home. I do not need to go to your house and do it."

He sat up and looked into her eyes.

"If you marry me I will bring you breakfast in bed every morning, and feed you the most delicious dainties and treats. I would dress you in the finest clothes, with rich silks and fabrics. Your stockings and shoes would be festooned with jewels. You would bathe in the finest soaps and perfumes, and move around in a grand carriage. We would travel the world and meet with kings and princes. I would love you and give you many children."

"I should like that," she said. "Having children."

His face was close to hers. Too close, but she could not move. He kissed her on the lips quickly, then laid his head back on her lap. She was stunned. He had taken her by surprise. She had the presence of mind not to turn her head to look in the direction of her stepmother. Hopefully, it had occurred so quickly that her chaperone had not noticed, or would not be sure what she saw.

Hours passed but neither of them wanted to leave. It was so peaceful that they fell asleep. Giuliano was woken some time later, being gently shaken by his driver.

"Signore," the servant said. "The Signora has become tired and wants to go. Please come."

"Si," answered the young Medici startled. "We will be right down."

Lisa woke up as well, surprised she had fallen asleep.

"This is how I want to wake up every morning," said Giuliano, sneaking a quick kiss on the lips again. "Seeing you."

Lisa wanted to kiss him back but could see her stepmother staring up at them. She was almost sorry Giuliano had brought the carriage and they hadn't gone off alone somewhere to kiss and hug. Her beau wanted to profess his love for her formally, however. She could hardly believe she was going to marry this marvelous, beautiful young man.

Caterina di Mariotto was also pleased at the way events were unfolding. She and her husband, Anton, could not have wished for a better match for Lisa. Only in her wildest dreams would she have let herself imagine something like this. Now it was actually about to occur. It would change their lives. What the boy's father, Lorenzo, and

Caterina's father's family, the Rucellai, thought about it, however, was another matter. She could only hope it would come to pass.

Her young cousin appeared serious enough. He was no alley cat to prowl at night and hide in the day. He was coming right out and announcing his intentions in the light of day for all to see. Lisa's stepmother would have waited all day for them, so as not to interrupt their romance, but it would be dark soon. To be out like this after dark would never do.

She only prayed that nothing would get in the way of their marriage.

Chapter 7 – Lorenzo's Ban

After bringing Lisa and her stepmother home, Giuliano lingered in their small courtyard talking to Lisa. The siblings and mother watched not so discreetly from the front windows. The young ones giggled and made snide remarks. The stepmother looked on with bated breath. They seemed like two people in love, which made her heart glad.

As it grew dark, Giuliano bowed and bid his sweetheart a fond adieu. With each passing moment together his heart grew more under her spell. For that is what it seemed like to the love-stricken youth. He was as if bewitched. Anton, Lisa's father, was too proud to appear concerned about such things. He ignored them all and feigned interest in a new sickle his neighbor had just bought.

Giuliano had ridden his horse to Lisa's house with the carriage, and had tied it behind on their little jaunt. He now mounted it and headed to the eastern part of the city and the family villa in Florence. They had many such buildings in Italy, but this one had been home to Cosimo, the founding father of the family. It had a special significance to them. Lorenzo, Giuliano's father, would be there this evening. Giuliano had important things to discuss with him.

The Villa of Careggy, as it was known, was situated on a slight rise surrounded by trees and exotic plants. The pale-yellow, three-story building looked like a castle, with large, ornate windows and an upper-story loggia. Behind the villa was a spacious, walled garden with plants and trees from all over the world.

His father was waiting for him in the library. Although only forty-three, Lorenzo had had a hard life. Known as the Magnificent, he had reigned for twenty-two years. Most of those years had been peaceful, but he had not earned his name by being a docile, mild ruler. Besides being an extravagant jouster and sportsman, he drank heavily and caroused with women, burning both ends of the candle, as they say. His hard living and bad diet had caught up with him, as had an infection in his leg caused by the gout.

"Ah, Giuliano," he said, when his son finally appeared before him. "I have been waiting for you. You took the carriage out today, I hear. Where did you go?"

"That is what I wanted to speak to you about, Father," answered Giuliano, talking rapidly. "But you have been so busy I have not had the chance."

"I have not been well," his father informed him. "I have been feeling poorly for the past few days."

"I am sorry, Father. What is the matter?"

"It is the damned pain in my leg and my fingers. I cannot write. I can barely hold a pen. Forget trying to wield a sword."

"Hopefully you will not be doing much sword fighting any time soon."

"One never knows with the French and the Borgia pope, but I am tired to death. I feel an attack coming on. I have sent for the physician."

"Hopefully, it is not serious and will pass. We need you with us now more than ever. You are the savior of our city."

"It is kind of you to say that, Giuliano, but you and your brother will soon be rulers of Florence. My days are numbered."

"Do not say that," objected his son.

"That is why it is important that you and Piero work together and be ready to succeed me. I assume you took the carriage to impress some maiden?"

"Si, Father."

"You would not need a carriage for that unless you wanted to impress her parents also. You must understand that you cannot carry on a serious affair without my approval. I have big plans for you. You must not interfere with them and marry against my wishes. You have no say in the matter."

"But, Father, I have met this girl. We have fallen in love. I want to marry her."

"No, that is totally out of the question."

"But you don't even know who it is."

"It does not matter."

"She is our cousin, Caterina di Mariotto's step-daughter, Lisa. Caterina married Antonmaria di Noldo Gherardini. They are an old noble family."

"They are a minor branch of the Rucellai family, of no importance. You will marry the King of Naples's daughter or the Duke of Savoy's."

'But, Father, Lisa has all the charm and intelligence of any of these girls. She would be an asset to any man, fit for any society. She is no farmer's daughter, or the daughter of a commoner. Meet her. You will see."

"You do not understand, Giuliano! Ah, I fear your brother Piero is no wiser. You have a duty to your family. You must carry on our traditions. We are rulers of a great city, yet we have no hereditary titles nor do we hold office. We work behind the scenes with other rulers, kings and dukes, popes and princes. We do this through treaties of honor and peace, which are achieved through marriage. Who you wed is of vital importance to your city, to its very survival. It cannot be left to chance, or to this thing you call love. It is extremely important, Giuliano. My decision is final!

"Do not meet or talk to this girl again. And do not think you can do it without my notice. The entire city is my eyes and ears. You cannot evade them. If you do, I will disown you. You will be out on the street, starving and begging. Or worse, you will end up in prison or banished. So do not dare to cross me on this. Do you understand, Giuliano?"

"Si, Father. I understand and will do as you command. May I go now?"

"Go, I am growing faint. Call the physician. Physician! Physician! I am feeling weak, Giuliano. The room twirls around me. Physician!"

Chapter 8 – Hope's End

Giuliano left his father in a state of agitation. The old man's orders went against every fiber of his being, but how could he disobey the great Lorenzo the Magnificent? He never should have told him. What was he thinking? He should have known. He'd heard it enough times. There was no one to blame but himself.

He burned his arm on a candle in self-anger. He burnt it black and now it hurt too much for him to sleep. So he stole out of the villa and made his way to Lisa's house.

He walked for two hours through the dark, narrow streets, but the time passed quickly for him in his troubled state. He cursed his father and his fate. How could he live without her? How would he survive with her? He pondered a way out of his dilemma but could find none. He had to obey his father or he would be an outcast, no use to Lisa or himself.

Perhaps he could run away with her, but where could they go? How would they live? On what? Where? He had to at least see her one more time. Tell her what his father had said.

He finally arrived at the Gherardini villa. Even this normally noisily neighborhood was quiet and deserted at this time of night. He crept up to her window in the back of the house and called her name. The window was open but there was no response. He threw a pebble up to attract her attention. A gruff male voice called out.

"Who is that? What do you want? What are you doing there?"

It was Lisa's father.

"It is I, Giuliano de Medici," he answered brazenly. "I wish to speak to Lisa."

"Sorry, my lad," said Anton rather submissively. He did not want to interfere in any way with the blossoming affair. "I will send her right down. Do not disturb yourself, Signore."

A few moments later, Lisa, only half awake, her eyes still partly shut, came down to the courtyard in her robe. Her mother and father listened intently from the upstairs window.

"Who is it?" Anton's wife asked him.

"It is the Medici boy," he answered. "He has come to talk to Lisa."

"At this late hour?" she said. "I hope there is nothing wrong. He was going to talk to Lorenzo tonight."

"Let us hope not," replied her husband, "but only another confession of love."

"I hope he does not want her to run away with him," the wife said, almost to herself. "I had a feeling Lorenzo would not go for it."

"He better not try to run away with Lisa!" replied Antonmaria. "I would impale him on a cross-bow beam."

Giuliano was standing in the courtyard under an olive tree when Lisa entered.

"What is it, Giuliano, that brings you here so late? Or should I say early, for the sun will be up soon."

"I need to talk to you, my sweet," he replied.

"I hope nothing is wrong," she said.

"I talked to my father. He forbade me to see you again. I have left the villa against his will. If he caught me he would put me in prison."

"That is terrible, my love," she said in distress. "You must do as he commands."

"No, you must come away with me. We can go to Venice. I have a place there, and friends."

"No, Giuliano, I cannot. I love you but I must stay and help my family. I cannot leave them like this. It would not be right. How would they survive?"

"I will take care of them," replied the earnest young aristocrat.

"How, if you are disowned or imprisoned? What would your father do to us? No, I could not leave my family like that. You were supposed to help us. Now what will become of us? Please, do not leave Florence, Giuliano. Do what your father says. Things may turn out all right, who knows. I will love you and cherish you in my heart no matter where you are. Be safe and take your place here by your family. Remember me."

"No, Lisa, I cannot be without you now that I have found you. It would be like living without a heart, like living in a bland, colorless world without smell or taste, a life not worth living."

"It will be life and that is better than death, my love. As long as you are breathing there is hope. I trust God wants us to be together. He will find a way. Pray and believe and it will happen."

"I wish I had your faith," he said.

"Go back to your father," she urged him. "Send me word when you can so I know you are well. Maybe we can meet in the Piazza some time. I would be happy just to hold your hand."

"I will not be happy if I cannot hold you like I held you that night and caress you with kisses."

"Oh, Giuliano, do not say such things. You make me faint."

He went to hold her around the waist but there was a loud grunt from above. Someone rapped a cane against a pan.

"We must be careful," Lisa warned him. "You should go. You do not want to be found away on the morrow."

"I will send word to you," he told her. "Do not worry. I love you."

"And I you. Farewell."

She bid him good-bye not knowing if she would ever see him again. Her future, which had seemed so certain and grand only a few hours before, was now filled with doubt. Her love, which had been so immediate and intense, now hung in the air like a thin mist blown away by the wind.

Chapter 9 – The Proclamation

Giuliano returned to the villa just as the cock began to crow. Despite the early hour, his older brother was there in the front room waiting for him.

"Where have you been, Giuliano," asked Piero, Lorenzo's eldest son and heir.

"I was out with some friends," he lied. "It is carnival time."

"Are you sure it was not this Lisa Gherardini you were out with?"

"What business is it of yours, Piero? You are not my keeper."

"Father is dead," said his eldest sibling without preamble.

"What?" said Giuliano. In shock, he almost fell to the ground. Recovering, he sat unsteadily on a nearby divan. "That cannot be. I just talked to him this evening. It cannot be."

"It is so. He is gone, I'm afraid. I went to get you so you could be with him, but you were not here. No one knew where you were, but father."

"I am sorry. I should have been here with him."

"So tell me then, Giuliano. Were you with that Gherardini girl tonight? After father told you not to see her again?"

"How do you know what father told me? That is not true. You were not there."

"It is so true. Father said as much on his death bed. Of all the things on his mind at the moment of death, he was most worried about you and that girl. You are meant for much more important things, things critical to the state, to our great city. You must do as he commanded. These are dangerous times but also times of great opportunity."

"I have no care for diplomatic matters. I will live my own life as I see fit."

"No, Giuliano, if you want to live well and prosper, you will do like I and the family tell you to. I carry on father's legacy and you will do as I say. You will not leave the villa. The guards have orders to stop you if you try. Do you understand?"

Giuliano did not answer but stormed out of the room.

Listen as they might out the upstairs window at Lisa and Giuliano's conversation that night, her father and stepmother could not hear the details of what was said. However, they could tell by Lisa's demeanor when she returned to the house that things had not gone well. The thirteen-year-old would tell them nothing, no matter how much they cajoled, threatened, and begged.

"How can we help you if you do not tell us what is the matter?" her stepmother said.

"Did something happen?" inquired her father. "What did the boy say?"

Lisa did not reply.

The following day, she sat unmoving and stared out the window without saying a word. Her face was immobile, her mind an empty slate. A faint, sad smile played on her lips. She looked as if she was thinking of a long-dead lover.

Anton wrung his hands. His wife, Caterina, cried into her apron. All seemed lost. Then, around noon, a carriage drove up to the front courtyard. It brought fresh hope. Maybe things were not lost yet. Perhaps a rapprochement was in sight. They rushed out with anticipation.

A small crowd had gathered, as on the previous day, neighbors and local shopkeepers eager and curious to learn what big event was unfolding. Something big must be happening because the carriage was obviously from someone of importance and wealth.

The occupant of the carriage stood but did not get out. The man was in the uniform of a captain of the guards and he addressed Antonmaria formally, reading from a paper he held out in front of him.

"Antonmaria di Noldo Gherardini, hear this. You and all of your household, but specifically your daughter Lisa, are hereby ordered to cease and desist from all meetings, correspondence, and contact with Giuliano de Medici under pain of imprisonment, as well as confiscation of all property in the city and surrounding country. You and your family are forbidden to contact Giuliano de Medici in person, at his home, at his work, at the council, by mail, or through a third party, no matter where he may reside or be located. Such contact would be a violation of this injunction and punishable by the laws of this domain. All persons from the Gherardini family must stay a hundred meters from Giuliano de Medici if encountering him on the street or Plaza. There is no exception to this rule, may God be our judge, by order of Piero de Medici, ruler of Florence."

Anton did not know what to expect and was hoping it might be an invitation to a ball or court. This was the worst thing that could have happened. Not only was he banished from having any contact with the

Medici, it was done in public before all his neighbors and friends. The humiliation was almost too much to bear.

He turned ashen gray and cast his eyes down, as the man in the carriage sat down and it pulled way. Those witnessing the scene, if they were friends of Anton, turned away in shame. Those who did not like the man or held some grudge or other against him, looked at him with malicious grins and laughed.

Lisa was aware of none of this, but held her seat at the rear window. She was a thousand miles away and as many years, in a world of her own making, where she and Giuliano played in fields of wildflowers and clover.

Chapter 10 – Shut-ins

Giuliano spent most of his days in the lush walled gardens that surrounded the Medici Villa Careggy. As his brother promised, he was watched continually. A watch-dog of Piero's sat not far from him under a tree at this very moment.

"This imprisonment is intolerable," he complained to his brother Giovanni. Giovanni was four years older than Giuliano and an ally. "It is not right that Piero treats me so."

"He is busy seeing to affairs of state. He takes his business seriously," his brother replied.

"As do I," said Giuliano. "I will not be treated like this. I have done nothing wrong."

"I agree, Giuliano, but how can I help you? You know Piero will not listen to me."

"Then mother must talk to him."

"Whose? His is gone. He will not listen to yours."

"There must be someone."

"Be patient," urged Giovanni. "In the meantime, perhaps I can talk to our uncle, Giuliano. He may be willing to help. Things may change. In any case, you have a beautiful villa in which to bide your time in."

"Bah, I am sick of it. A prison by any other name is still a prison. I must be rid of it."

"And where would you go if you were free of it?" asked Giovanni.

"I would go to see Lisa," Giuliano answered.

"See, there you are. That is why you are kept here under guard. Forget her, my brother. You are meant for grander things."

"That is what everyone says, but I love Lisa. She is grander than all the daughters of kings put together."

"I hear Piero is courting Cesare Borgia. His sister is supposed to be very beautiful."

"I would not marry that man's sister no matter if he was king of all Europe and she a beauty beyond compare. She would still not be as pretty as my Lisa."

"Ah, I do not envy you, Giuliano. That is why I chose the priesthood."

"Yes, you will be Pope some day, I am sure."

"Aye, too bad I am not Pope now. I could grant you a dispensation."

"What is that?" asked Giuliano.

"It would lift you from Piero's ban and allow you to marry your sweetheart."

"Oh, that you were Pope, my brother, oh that you were Pope."

Days turned to weeks. Weeks turned to months. Still, Lisa did not move from her spot in front of the second story back window. Her parents had given up trying to talk to her, although they did ask the parish priest for help. He came and went with little apparent success, although he did sprinkle holy water on her.

Her stepmother gave her sponge baths from time to time and the physician prescribed a purgative, with blood-letting. It was all to no effect. She ate but little. The bits of bread and raw vegetables left overnight were gone by morning, although no one saw her eat them. They could just as well have been taken by the birds. She remained thin and gained no weight.

The only thing that seemed to entertain her was her younger siblings playing and yelling to each other in the courtyard below. When a ball was thrown to her, however, or her name called in fun, she did not respond, but sat like one deaf and dumb. It was troubling, to say the least, and all of them, siblings and parents alike, were concerned but helpless.

They had heard nothing of the Medici boy and were petrified to inquire. They lived their lives in fear, shunned by their neighbors and friends for being banished from the sight of such a rich and important family. Lisa's father labored heavily under the shame of it.

"We must do something about Lisa," he told his wife one night. "We must get her married soon or we are doomed."

"I would be happy if she talked and laughed again," said her stepmother. "Perhaps a change of scenery would help. I was thinking of taking her to the country."

"That is a good thought," replied Anton. "It will be time to harvest the wheat soon. We will take her to the farm at St. Donato, to the Ca' di Pesa in Poggio."

"Si, the change will be good for her," insisted her stepmother. "She will be outside. She will get her color back. There is nothing like good country air."

"Hopefully she will get more back than her color," said Anton.

"I'm afraid without her Giuliano, she will get naught back."

"Then we are doomed," lamented Anton.

"What are we to do?" Caterina asked.

"We certainly cannot let her see the Medici boy again. Maybe we can marry her off to a rich merchant."

"The news of her rejection and Lorenzo's ban must be known by all. Where would we find someone who knows naught of it?"

"Or who does not care," replied Anton.

"A foreigner maybe," said Caterina.

"Perhaps an older man or widower."

"Si, there are enough of them but will he be rich and generous?"

Chapter 11 – Rebellion

It was a hot day. The Tuscan sun burnt through the morning haze and scorched the mountainsides. Giuliano found his brother in the second-floor loggia, fanning himself and drinking chilled Chianti.

"Piero, I have been looking all over for you," said Giuliano. "No one would tell me where you were."

"I did not want to be disturbed. I was resting. It is so cool up here with the breeze and such a nice view. I needed to rest. I have been so busy since father died."

"Yes, I know. I wish there was more that I could do," replied Giuliano.

"You are doing what our father would have wanted by staying away from that girl. I am sorry that I have to keep you here. It is for your own good."

"It is for your perverted idea of family honor. Do not pretend that you do this for me. I cannot bear such hypocrisy."

"Watch your words, Giuliano. The French are restless," Piero told him. "They make noise and rattle their swords."

"And what do we do, cower in our boots?"

"We marry them and have them breed our fat babies. That is how kings are made."

"That is how bitches are bred, not me. I will be my own man."

"Do you want to rule Florence one day?"

"I care not," replied Giuliano.

"Well, I do care. I will govern it the way I see fit and you will do as I say."

"You are too subservient to the French. Everyone complains. Be careful you don't become their bitch."

"You be careful of what you say, Brother. I put up with your lack of respect, but I will not put up with your insults. It would be foolish to antagonize the French. Their army is twice the size of ours. Our countrymen all fight among themselves. It would be folly to go to war with them."

"They will devour us if we do nothing, like so much cabbage in a field."

"That is why it is important to make good treaties of peace, and the best way to do that is through marriage. We need strong allies."

"I will not be a pawn in your games."

"These are not games we play in, Giuliano, but survival. Milan, Pisa, Genoa, Naples, they all struggle to carve a place for themselves. We must do the same."

"I want no part of this."

"I am sorry, Brother, but we have no choice. God has decided our place in life and we must do his bidding the best we know how."

"I cannot believe father is gone like that," said Giuliano with anguish in his voice.

"Would it have made any difference? It would not have changed your fate."

"No, I suppose not. I would still be separated from my Lisa. I fear that is something I will have to get used to."

"I will need you, Giuliano," said his brother.

"You have Giovanni. He is a good sort."

"He has chosen the religious path."

"Do not underestimate the power of religion."

"I do not, but as far as marriages go, except for performing them, a priest will be of no service to us."

"Yes, brother," said Giuliano. "I want to be of service to our family and live up to the examples of our grandfather, Cosimo, and our father. But it is hard sometimes, when you find love and lose it all at the same time."

"Do not dwell on it, Giuliano. Perhaps a time will come when you can have a dalliance with the girl, but not now. Now is a critical time. Until we can figure out how to deal with the French everything will be uncertain."

"Just be careful that you do not give away too much for peace or you will not rule for long."

"I will rule long enough, do not worry. Just rule your impulses and all will be well."

"You have your concubines," Giuliano declared. "Why should not I?"

"Because the time is not good," replied Piero. "As I said, we need to keep you in reserve in case a strategic alliance presents itself. In the meantime, you can help me govern the city. I want you to start attending the council meetings. You need to become familiar with factions in the government and how they align."

"I already am. That is why I have warned you about becoming too cozy with the French. None of the factions like it. They all fear the French king's influence."

41

"He will either have influence over us or have our city itself, I am afraid, if we are not careful. What do you suggest I do?"

"Tread carefully, and let me see Lisa," insisted Giuliano. "I will be discreet. No one will know."

"What? You joke with your older brother. Do you seek to make me laugh?"

"No, I ..."

"Her parents would know," Pierro explained. "Their friends and neighbors would know. It would cause a scandal and interfere with things, make everything more complicated. In any case, the girl may not want to be your concubine and raise your illegitimate children. I thought you loved her."

"I do and I want to be with her," answered Giuliano.

"You would ruin her name to do it?" Pierro inquired.

"We could find a husband for her that would play along," said his younger brother.

"I forbid you to see this girl," demanded Piero. "If you do, she and her family will be banished along with you. The quicker I can see you are over her, the quicker things can get back to normal for you."

"Things will never get back to normal for me," said Giuliano dejectedly.

"I have decided. There is someone I want you to meet," Piero said. "She is a beauty. Her family is quite important. I will arrange it. Her name is Lucrezia and she will make you forget all about this Gherardini girl."

Chapter 12 – A Conduit

Giuliano remained in his sumptuous prison, locked away from the world by his brother for fear of his love for a young girl. Try as he might, he had been unable to elude his guards and escape from the villa, although he had attempted to several times.

He had a visitor. It was his uncle.

"Giovanni has told me of your plight," said his father's brother, Giuliano, who had agreed to help him. "I could have one of my people take a note to your Lisa if you like, and set up a meeting. Our cousin, Caterina, would not know."

"That would be a wonder," replied Lorenzo's third son, with the same name as his uncle. "Even better if you could arrange for me to leave the villa and actually see her."

"That might be possible," said the elder Giuliano de Medici, "under the right circumstances. It might be difficult here in the city, but I understand they are going to their farm in the country soon. I plan to take a little trip to the south myself. Perhaps we could arrange for you to come with me and meet her there."

"That would be fantastic," said Giuliano the younger. "Perhaps there is hope after all."

"Ah, there is always hope, my nephew. As long as you are breathing and awake, there is always hope."

"You must contact Lisa directly, not through her parents. Anton and Caterina must not know. I do not know how they would take it, since my father sent a sergeant at arms to ban contact with them."

"I will contrive to contact Lisa directly, if possible."

"Good. Then it is settled. I will wait for your word. Thank you, Uncle."

"Giovanni, your brother, has told me how unjust Piero has been. There is no reason your love must die if the girl is willing to continue seeing you, but you must be honest with her, marriage is impossible."

"Perhaps for now, but who knows what the future brings," said Giuliano.

The wheat harvesting season was upon them, but Lisa's family had yet to move to the farm in Poggio. Everyone was ready but Lisa. She refused to move from the second-story window. Anton was considering tying her to the wagon and carrying her there, although that meant the newborn lamb would have to somehow walk.

Then one morning, when the whole family and the servant had gone to market, there was a knock on the back door. This was followed by a pebble hitting the second-floor window pane. This got Lisa's attention. She rose and opened the window to see a boy dressed in livery

"Can I be of service?" she asked.

"Is your name Lisa?" the boy inquired.

"Yes, it is. Who wants to know?"

"Please, Signora, are you alone here? Is there anyone else about?"

"I will not tell you if I am alone or not, but I will tell you that you can say what you want without fear."

"Signora, I am sent from Giuliano. He tells you he is well and misses you. He wants to see you. He will be near St. Donato in Poggia in three days time. I understand your father has a farm there."

"Si," she replied.

"Be there on this Thursday next and he will find you. Be alone. Can you do this?"

"Si, tell Giuliano I will be there "

With that the messenger was gone.

The transformation was astounding. Overnight, Lisa changed from an unkempt recluse to a clean, vibrant girl, who couldn't wait to go to the country. She was talkative and ate with the rest of the family for the first time in weeks. She talked excitedly about being in the country again and working in the fields. She did not mention that she was going to see her lover.

They left the next day. Lisa walked beside the wagon with her older siblings, either herding farm animals like goats and cows, or pushing a cart. The trip took most of the day. The seasonal migration to the country was looked forward to by all, although there was always hard work involved.

Besides the wheat, which had to be harvested with sickles and bound together in baskets, there were grapevines to be tended and wine to press. Cows needed to be milked and sheep sheared. The single farmhand who watched the place off season kept the house and grounds clean but did minimal farm work, just enough to tend the animals.

She helped set up house on their arrival and assisted her stepmother with dinner, acting as if nothing had happened in the months she had sat comatose at the upstairs window.

"How are you feeling today?" asked Caterina.

"Fine, thank you," replied Lisa. "It is great to be out in the country."

"Have you heard from Giuliano," her stepmother inquired.

"What?" said Lisa in alarm, as if her stepmother had uttered a terrible curse.

"Your father has been unhinged by the Medicis' ban," Caterina went on, not persisting in her questioning. "It has upset him greatly. Look how it affected you. It is good to see you are your old self again. It is well we are out of the city and away from things. Now we can work and get back to normal."

"Yes, it will be good to be in the country again," agreed Lisa, counting down the moments until she would see Giuliano again.

Chapter 13 – Poggio

On the day she was to meet Giuliano, Lisa told her parents she was going to the local monastery to get honey. She would be back before dark, she informed them, as it was several miles distant. Then she stole away to the rendezvous spot, a secluded meadow no longer used. Sitting on a hillside, she picked wildflowers to give him.

A great feeling of peace came over her at the thought of seeing him. The field was covered with yellow and white flowers. The hills receded in the distance like fields of mist. White wispy clouds floated in a sea of clear blue air.

She wore a dark peasant blouse with long pleated sleeves, under a light, flowing, mustard-colored smock. It billowed in the breeze. Her long, dark hair fell loosely down her back, curling at the ends.

Looking up, she saw a figure approaching across the field. It was just a vague form at first, hardly recognizable as a person at all. With each passing minute, however, as the form walked doggedly toward her, more and more came into focus.

She recognized that gait - the swaying of the shoulders, the stamp of the legs, the long, determined stride. It was Giuliano! She rose with a yell of joy and ran toward him, clutching the bouquet of wildflowers in her hand.

He wore a short, richly-colored tunic, which only came to his thighs, and black tights that showed off his long, muscular legs. A purple cape hung over his shoulder.

As Lisa came bounding to him like a gazelle, Giuliano stopped and spread his arms as if to catch her. She ran to him without slowing and met him at full speed.

Throwing her arms up, she leapt in the air. Luckily for them both, Giuliano was not only agile, he was strong. He had also seen acrobats and dancers do the move, though he had never tried it himself – until now.

As she leaped he caught her under the arm, and bringing his other arm beneath her, spun her around. He let her momentum carry them through several turns before gently putting her feet on the ground. She kissed him repeatedly – a thousand times he would say recounting it later. He held her tight and showered her face with kisses in return.

"As you instructed me," she said when he paused. "I told my parents that I was going to the monastery to buy honey."

"Good," he answered. "I have some here to give you."

"We have until supper time," she explained. "Then I must part."

"Then we have no time to waste," he said, kissing her again.

"Oh, Giuliano, it is like a dream to be with you. How did you manage it? I have so much to tell you. I have missed you so."

"And I you. Ah, you look so good," he said. "I could devour you. I trust this is a private spot."

"No one comes here," she answered. "They are all working in the wheat fields."

"It will not matter," said Giuliano, taking off his cape and spreading it on the ground. "Here, sit."

He pulled her down to the cape with him as he sat.

"The tall grass will hide us."

Saying this, he lay down and rested her head on his arm. Putting the other arm over her, he kissed her hard. She had never been horizontal with a man before. She found the experience dizzying and sat up quickly.

"You make me dizzy!" she said.

Giuliano laughed.

"I am sorry," he said. "I am so anxious to be with you. I have dreamed of this moment so many times."

"What kind of dreams have you been having?" she asked him. "I have been dreaming too, but not like this. I am not a country maid. You have promised to marry me, my prince. I am yours to wed, not to seduce."

"I am sorry, Lisa. I must be honest with you. My father forbade me to see you again, but he has died. My brother has continued the ban and sent his men to inform your family. It would be very bad for them if he were to find out we were together. I am a pawn in his grand schemes. There is nothing I can do. Come away with me. Come away with me this instant. We can go to France or perhaps England, where there is more freedom and less petty tyrants."

"But you must know I cannot leave my parents," she told him. "They need me. I must marry or they will be destitute. If you cannot marry me, than I must marry another, if you have not already ruined me."

"I have not ruined you. Go marry another, but do not forsake me."

Pulling her down again, he leaned over her, resting his body on hers. As he talked, Lisa became more aware of him pressing against her. He looked better the closer he got. His skin was smooth and flawless, his dark eyes deep and piercing. She longed to have his long fingers and beautiful hands on her. He was so close. She could see the longing in his eyes. He kissed her again passionately.

"Let us enjoy each other now," he said, "for we may not have another moment such as this."

He opened the basket he had brought and took out a loaf of bread and a flask of brandy, pulling out the cork with his knife. Taking a metal cup, he poured some, took a sip, and gave the cup to her. They shared it back and forth many times as they nibbled on the bread.

"You are mine, my sweetheart, my mystery girl, who hid her name from me but gave me her heart. I will never give it back, for you stole mine that first night. You left me a half a man. Now I am only whole when I am with you. I am empty without you. When we are apart all I do is think of being with you again. I cannot live like this. If I cannot have you I shall die. But if I can be with you, only for moments like this, I might yet survive with the hope that I might see you again."

He brushed away the hair that had fallen to her face and spread it in his fingers. It felt and shined like fine silk. He held her ribs and stuck his thumb in her stomach near her navel like a tiger clawing its prey. Covering her mouth with his, he drew the breath from her. She died in his arms as something exploded in her.

His mouth went to her neck, where his lips and teeth played on the pulsing veins of her throat. Pulling the neck of her blouse down just enough to expose the top part of a white, budding breast, he kissed it fervently. She exploded again, seeing stars and wiggling white lines fly by in the periphery of her vision.

Giuliano also exploded in ecstasy, staining his black, bulging tights. Everything stopped. The world stood still. All sounds ceased. They fell asleep in each other's arms.

Chapter 14 – The Storm

"Where could she be?" said Lisa's stepmother. "She should have been home long ago. It is past supper time and dark."

"She said she was going to the monastery to get some of their produce," replied Anton. "Perhaps she decided to stay because of the storm."

"She would never stay out like this, unless something was wrong. Maybe she is hurt."

"Well, there is nothing we can do now," said Anton. "But wait until morning when the storm is over."

"She could be lying out there somewhere hurt. Perhaps you and the boys should go out looking for her."

"No, we might lose the boys if we get trapped in the storm. It is dark in any case and the monastery is a good way off. No, I am sure she is all right. She might come home at any time. It would be foolish to go off blindly looking for her like that."

"Well, just sitting here doing nothing is harder than going out into the storm," said Caterina.

"Humph, that is easy enough for you to say. You would not be the one going out," replied Anton.

When his wife said nothing, he asked her a question that had been on his mind since that afternoon.

"How was it that your cousin came by today?"

"He is touring the district to raise money for the bishop."

"Why? Does not the church have enough money?" her husband said.

"My cousin is very conscientious in its service."

"He is Lisa's suitor, Giuliano's uncle, is he not?"

"Yes. What of it?" inquired his wife.

"You don't suppose he was here on his nephew's behalf do you?"

"What? You mean as a messenger to Lisa? No, the idea is … I don't know," she said after further consideration.

"It is odd that he shows up and she does not come home," said Anton. "It would go hard for us if Giuliano is meeting Lisa behind Piero's back. We have been warned with the most dire consequences."

"No," answered his wife. "Even if Giuliano wanted to try something like that, my cousin would not go along. He is a religious man. He would not go against Piero in any case."

"Would he not? These Medici are ruthless and powerful opportunists. They get what they want, all of them. We must be careful your cousins do not ruin our daughter with their intrigues. We must protect her and ourselves."

"Oh, where could she be?" lamented Lisa's stepmother.

Lisa was jarred awake when a bolt of lighting lit up the sky. It was followed by a loud peal of thunder that would have wakened her even if the blinding flash had not. Her lover woke up as well.

It was dark, the moon and stars blocked by thick storm clouds. It had started to rain. As she looked into the darkened sky, another burst of lighting momentarily blinded her. It was soon followed by a booming thunderclap that exploded nearby, shaking the ground. The wind and rain picked up into a gale.

"We have slept too long," said Giuliano. "A storm is upon us. Quickly, we must find shelter."

"There is an old hay barn at the top of the hill," Lisa told him. "We used to keep hay there for the sheep. It is falling down and not used anymore, but it might provide some protection from the rain."

"Please lead the way before we get soaking wet," said Giuliano. "I, for one, am not dressed for this weather."

"Nor I," she replied as she started up the hill. Giuliano ran beside her, holding his cape over their heads like a large umbrella, the basket in his other hand.

It was hard running up the hill in the darkness. The long grass tugged at their feet. The wind and rain lashed their faces. They stumbled over rough turf, rocks, and ditches. Lightning thrashed the sky. Thunder reverberated through the hills. Their clothes were soaked by the time the old building appeared suddenly before them in the mist as if it had popped out of thin air.

The roof and beams were mostly gone. Only remnants of the stone walls stood like silent pillars against the sky. But a portion of the building remained upright, enough for a horse or two to stand in. It was all the room they needed to shelter from the storm.

A partial roof covered their heads. There were even a couple bales of hay in the corner.

"This will do until the storm lets up," said Giuliano looking around.

"I wonder what my poor parents are saying now," said Lisa. "They must be worried. It is late."

"Perhaps they think you are at the monastery still, as you told them."

"I hope they do not go out looking for me."

"Do they know about this place?"

"Yes, of course, it has been in our family all my life."

"Then perhaps they reasoned you have come here. If so, they must know you are safe and will not worry."

"Maybe you should go," said Lisa. "They may come here looking for me. They might catch us. That would not be good."

"Why not? They know that I love you."

"They also know that you cannot marry me, that I have been forbidden, under the severest penalties, from seeing you. Do not put them through that."

"They would not come out tonight."

"I do not know."

"I do not want to leave you," he said, "not on a night such as this, not alone."

She was about to object when she heard the loud howling of a wolf. It sounded close by, as if it was right outside their dilapidated shelter.

"What was that?" she asked loudly as another wolf answered with a howl of its own. As most Florentines, Lisa was petrified of wolves.

"A couple of wolves are nearby," observed Giuliano. "They will not bother us."

"How do you know?" said Lisa. "They sound pretty hungry to me. They sound like they are right outside the barn. Do you have a weapon?"

"I have a small knife," he said, taking it from the sheath at his side. "But it would not do if I have to meet one face on. A heavy club or stick would do better. I could find one if I had better light, but I would have to search the grounds. I can make better use of my knife to make a fire."

"You can do that?" she asked anxiously.

"Yes, if my flint piece is still with me and dry."

The two wolves turned out to be a pack of a half dozen. For some reason they were attracted to the old dilapidated structure and began to surround it. They were getting more emboldened as their numbers increased. Big and well-fed, they started to probe the barn. The noise that Giuliano and Lisa made to scare the animals away only seemed to draw them closer and spur them on.

Giuliano checked a pouch in his tunic and pulled out a piece of flint he used, like most Florentines, to light fires. Taking his knife and a few pieces of hay, he struck the knife to the flint several times. The sparks ignited the hay, which, put together with more hay and twigs, blazed into a full-fledged fire.

He found a solid stick of wood near by.

"Please, my love," he asked. "Could you tear a small piece off the bottom of your smock, just enough to make a torch? I will tie it onto the stick with some hay and soak it with what is left of the brandy in my flask. It should flare up nicely. I can use it to fend off any wolves that try to get in here."

She did as he asked, just in time!

As soon as Giuliano wrapped the cloth from Lisa's dress around the end of the wood, the biggest of the wolves braved their shelter. It came in snarling and growling, its hackles up and its teeth bared, low and crouching. Giuliano quickly doused the end of the stick with the alcohol and stuck it into the fire. The fumes of the warm drink ignited the rags. As the animal approached him ready to spring, he shoved the blazing torch into its snapping jaws.

The wolf howled and leaped back out of the barn. Giuliano chased after it and confronted another gray wolf crouching and baring its teeth. He waved the makeshift torch, which flickered and flared, back and forth in front of the animals face, scaring it.

When it turned to dart away, he jammed the flame onto its backside, catching its tail on fire. The wolf ran off yelping and howling, its flaming tail waving back and forth behind it. This apparition frightened the rest of the pack, which disappeared into the night.

It was still raining hard. The thunder and lightning had moved off to the north. Giuliano stood ready with his torch in case the wolves decided to return, but it looked like he had scared them off for good.

He built up the fire with the torch and pieces of wood from the barn's old roof. Once they felt safe and the fire was flaring well, Lisa and Giuliano took off their wet clothes. Hanging them on rafters close to the fire, they cuddled next to it and fell asleep, Giuliano in his breeches, Lisa in her chemise.

Chapter 15 – Lost and Found

Lisa woke to the sound of someone calling her name.

"Here she is!" the voice yelled.

It was her brother, Giovangual. She looked to where she expected her lover to be lying, but there was no one there. Giuliano was gone.

"Where have you been all night?" asked her father coming up to her. "We were so worried."

Lisa had been rehearsing her story the entire evening as she lay in her lover's arms. The feel of him as he enclosed her, each inch of his body pressed to her, felt so good, so secure that she never wanted him to let her go. It was as if she was shielded from all harm, from all evil in the world.

Where had he gone? Was he gone for good? When would he return? She wanted to scream out the questions. Instead, she told them she was in the field on her way home after visiting the monastery and got caught in the storm. She told them lightning had started the fire in the barn and that she had slept there all night protected from the storm. She did not tell them about the wolves or Giuliano.

She was like a starving person who had finally had a meal, like someone who had gone without water in the desert that finally had a drink. She was satiated, satisfied, filled with joy and love. Everything looked beautiful, radiating with a light that came from within her, from her elated soul.

She knew her love for Giuliano would never die, but burn within her breast like a living flame. Even more, she knew his love for her would outlast all of life's obstacles and burdens. It would be there in the end no matter what might happen.

She was no longer yearning, no longer empty, no longer seeking what she could not have. She had his love locked in her heart and it would never leave her. It would sustain her through hardship and sickness. It would keep her living, living with gratitude. She had loved and been loved. Better yet, she knew that was her reason for being here on earth.

Giuliano had quietly stolen away an hour before daylight, soon after the storm broke and the rain stopped. He looked at Lisa lying there asleep next to the fire for a long time, not taking his eyes off her. She looked so innocent and peaceful, so beautifully formed, with hair and skin so soft and alluring you couldn't help kissing it. He wanted so much to touch and hold her, put his lips to her breasts. Instead, he took his clothes and his cape, his basket and brandy flask, and erasing all evidence of his being there, left the dilapidated barn.

He made his way back to the hostel where he was staying with his uncle. Giuliano was a man of action. He wanted to take Lisa and run away. Fortunately, he was also a man of deliberation, wise for one his age.

Lorenzo had taught him well, as befitted one destined for leadership. Every action had a consequence. A wise man played the likely consequences of his actions in his mind before doing them, like looking ahead in a game of chess. This was smart, in case there were bad results from the action. It did not take Giuliano long to realize running away with Lisa would be disastrous for all involved.

After looking at his options it was obvious he had to go back to Piero and do as he said. But before that he would see her one more time.

He knew that whatever happened he had Lisa's love. She would be his no matter what. Nothing mattered as long as they loved each other. He thought about what he had promised her and wondered if he could actually bring himself to find a husband for her. Perhaps, but it would not be a high priority.

Chapter 16 – The Poems

Lisa continued to work on the harvest with her brothers and sisters, but something had changed in her. She stepped more lively. She sang to herself as she worked, always with a lazy smile on her lips. She spoke, but only when spoken to and always appeared as if daydreaming of some far away place.

Her parents were worried. Her story of what had happened to her in the storm was believable enough, but her change of attitude was harder to explain, especially when her situation was considered. The great hope they'd had when Giuliano was courting her had been crushed. Her future prospects had been squashed along with it.

Things were well enough in the country, away from the wagging tongues and prying eyes of the city, but that would end with the harvest season. They were scheduled to return to Florence at the end of the month, but nothing awaited the family there but rejection and shame.

"I have reached out to the family and all their connections for someone who knows of a likely suitor for Lisa," said her father. "Not one has responded. No one even answers me, let alone offers a name. It is like the subject is forbidden."

"Si, even my relations, which are wider than yours, can find no one," Lisa's stepmother replied. "The Medici have ruined us, but all is not lost. Forget the aristocracy, our landowning acquaintances. Forget about the city big-wigs. There are many rich merchants in Florence, commoners that would love to marry into an old family like ours."

He looked at her in shock. "Commoners!" Antonmaria said. "You cannot be serious."

"Yes, I am serious. These are desperate times, my dear."

"Then give me a name. How do I go about finding them?" asked her husband.

"I do not know. Perhaps one of them will find us," answered his wife.

A few days after her rendezvous with Giuliano, around dinner time, when the others were at the cottage eating, Lisa sneaked out to the field full of wildflowers where she had met Giuliano. The sun was shining. It was a clear autumn day.

She was strolling through the flowers, reliving their moments together, when she spotted the old hay barn at the top of the hill. Running up to it, she laid down in the hay where they had lain together.

Turning over onto her back, she looked up at the rafters and the remains of the roof. There, stuck between two boards, was a slip of paper. Standing, she took it from the wall.

It was a poem. She read it.

> *My love for you fills my heart.*
> *I long for you when we are apart.*
> *My love for you fills me with joy.*
>
> *I will nurture it like a hidden flower,*
> *Carry it until my final hour.*
> *My love for you is true and real.*
>
> *Tell me truest, will thou be mine?*
> *If so, I will love you 'til the end of time.*
> *I will not rest until you are mine.*

The poem was not signed. It was written in ink with a fine hand. Was it from Giuliano? Did he write it to her? What else could it be?

She read it again, then again and again, repeatedly until the fading light made reading too difficult. Then she tucked the poem under her skirt and made her way home.

All that night as she lay in bed, she clutched it to her heart, holding it as if it were an expensive and rare jewel. It meant more to her than any treasure. It was a token of his love, an emblem of their eternal bond. She kept it close to her at all times, waking, sleeping, and read it many times over when she was alone.

She longed to talk to him and tell him how she felt. Then one day, while she was tallying the bales of wheat, she took a blank sheet of paper and wrote this in pencil:

> *Wrapped in your embrace,*
> *The kindness of your face,*
> *The pleasure of your kiss,*
> *All gives me so much bliss,*
> *Remembering you,*
> *I long for you.*

Sticking it in a notch between the boards, she left it at the old barn, hoping Giuliano would somehow get her poem. She did not get a chance to return until the following week. To her disappointment, the piece of paper was still there. When she opened it to check it, however, she found it was not the poem she had written, but another. She read it.

> *I love you deeply, my love divine,*
> *I love you truly, you must be mine.*
> *No matter what the fates dictate,*
> *The tender love that we did make,*
> *Will forever be in my mind.*
> *I will love you 'til the end of time.*
> *Of one thing you may be sure,*
> *I will love you for evermore.*

Again, she pressed the paper to her breast as tears came to her eyes. She could hear his voice as she read the poem again aloud. She ran home with the slip of paper clutched to her bosom and hid it in her mattress so that she could read it over and over that evening, while alone in bed.

A week passed. She kept going back to the barn, but there were no notes, so she left one of her own hoping he would get it. It read:

> *Though I am not your wife,*
> *I will share your life.*
> *You make the minutes last as hours.*
> *You hold me captive with your powers.*
> *You give me the love that I need.*
> *My love for you no thing can exceed.*
> *You are so patient and kind.*
> *Oh, my dearest, please be mine.*
> *There is one thing you must know,*
> *Beyond all things, I love you so.*

She went back every day to see if there was a new poem. The paper was gone by the beginning of the following week, the last week of harvest. They would be returning to the city after the weekend, when the harvest festival picnic would occur.

Lisa visited the dilapidated barn on the last day before the festival. To her delight, there was a new note stuck in the crevice between the wall boards. Opening it, she read.

> *You are the flower of my garden,*
> *Which lies barren without you.*
> *My tears warm the morning dew.*
> *It is for no other, but only you.*
> *You are the sweet angel of my heart,*
> *All that I yearn for, all that I want*
> *You opened my rainbow,*
> *It bridges the sky,*
> *And fills it with grandeur,*
> *For our love will never die.*

She read it many times, more than all the others, for it touched her deeply. She cried each time she did. Rather than making her feel good, it made her feel empty with longing, while everyone around her was gay and happy in anticipation of the festival and dance.

Chapter 17 – The Harvest Dance

Lisa had elapsed back into sadness. She lay in bed all day, not getting up with the family, hardly eating. She had no joy in anything. She even lost interest in the yearling lamb she had been feeding and taking care of.

"How can you mope around like that with the dance tonight?" asked her stepmother. "All the boys in the district will be there."

Lisa did not answer.

"What is wrong with you, young lady?" Caterina continued. "Get out of bed. Wash your face. Put on clean clothes. I will not have you mope around all day."

"Why?"

"Because I say so, that is why. You are not so old I cannot take a strap to you. Do you not want to go to the dance?"

"No, I do not care a fig about the dance."

"Have you no interest in anything?"

"Only dying."

"Do not say such a thing. Life is a gift from heaven. It is a sin to think otherwise."

"I do not care. Life is not fair."

"You are not thinking of Giuliano are you? I thought you were over him. You have been so happy since we came here."

"It is because of him that I came and I was happy."

Lisa could keep the secret no longer. She had to tell someone.

"What?" said her mamma loudly.

"He was here. That is who I was with the night of the storm. We were together the whole night. We slept together."

"Then the boy must marry you. We will demand it."

"No, you cannot. It would mean our ruin and his. His brother would not stand for it. You must never speak of it to anyone, not even Papa."

"But you must. If you slept with him, you might be with child. Then what would you do?"

"It was not like that, Mamma. We just talked."

"But you will be ruined. Who will marry you now?" wailed Caterina

"That is why no one will know. You must keep this secret with me," pleaded Lisa.

"Is he still here? Where is Giuliano?"

"I have not seen him since that night," Lisa told her. "He must have gone back to Florence."

She did not tell her stepmother about the poems. She did not want to alarm her more than she already had.

"Promise me you will not see this boy again," Caterina begged.

"No, I cannot do that," said Lisa. "I love him."

"Oh, Lisa, what have you done?" her stepmother said, wringing her hands. "We will be ruined."

"No, Mamma. You must not worry. Trust me. All will be well."

Lisa's mood improved after talking to her mother. She washed, put on fresh clothes, and helped the others prepare food and decorations for the dance. Her mother's mood also changed, for the worse. She wore the worry and concern on her face all that day. Anton was in a festive mood, however, and hardly noticed.

That evening a large crowd gathered in the square at the center of the village of Poggio for the harvest dance. A small platform had been erected for the band of three - made up of lyre, flute, and tambourine - who kept up a lively beat.

The carpenters had laid down a temporary floor of shaved logs for the dancers. The guests stood in groups around it, or sat on benches and tables scattered about the square.

Lisa wandered along the periphery of the festivities, watching the people dance and celebrate, including her siblings, who made merry on a corner of the dance floor reserved for children.

The usual collection of locals was there, farmers and merchants, villagers and officials. They stood mostly in clumps and discussed business or gossiped. The young people sat on the benches, men on one side, women on the other.

No one had gotten up the nerve to ask anyone to dance yet. Only married couples made use of the floor. Most of the songs were round dances, like riddas and ballonchios. It wasn't until the band started up a rousing Righoletto that the young people started to move.

Even though a majority wore masks in the festive holiday spirit, Lisa wore none. Despite their disguises, she knew most of the people there. They had been coming to these seasonal events for many years. However, a group of four well-dressed young men, who showed up half way through the night, attracted her attention.

They didn't look or act like locals, but stayed to themselves. Most of those attending wore simple, coarse country clothes. These men wore elegant costumes more designed for court than a peasant dance. She wondered who they were. While she was pondering this, one of them walked up to her.

He wore a short black tunic with gold embroidery and mustard-colored tights. He had a purple cape with red highlights. He bowed at the waist.

"Vuoi ballare, Signorita?" he asked.

It took her but a minute to regain her composure and answer.

"Si, Signore, I would love to dance," she replied. She knew instantly who it was from his voice. As she took his hand and followed him to the dance floor, she asked, "Giuliano! What are you doing here?"

"Do not call me that!" he whispered. "No one must know I am here. Call me Carlo. I have come with some of my friends. You can tell everyone we are a band of travelers, seeing the world as required by our parents for our education. We are staying at the hostel."

She stood next to him holding his hand when the band started a jaunty round. Between singing, clapping, and shuffling their feet, they talked to each other.

"I cannot believe you are here," she said.

"Do not say too much," he suggested. "It might be best."

"There is so much I want to say. I love you so," replied Lisa.

"And I you, but tonight we dance. I promise you there will be other times."

They danced in circles, ran under bridges of arms, swayed in lines all to the music, some in triple time, some in two-four, others slow, many fast. They scampered together on the wooden floor all night.

At one point during a rapid air, Giuliano twirled her around for a dozen spins, until she was almost too dizzy to stand. Everyone clapped. She fell down laughing in his arms as she had that first night at the ball, although this time the countless stars were real.

Everyone wondered who the stranger dancing with Lisa was. She told them the story Giuliano told her to say. Her mother knew the truth. Her father suspected it.

The last song was a slow one. He faced her and bowed. She returned a curtsy. He then, ever so gently, took her left hand with his right and lifted it above their heads. As he did this, he stepped forward with his right foot, then back. She did the same. Then they daintily moved clockwise on tip-toes, so that they faced in the opposite direction. At this point, he bowed again, she curtsied, and they repeated the whole process, ending back where they started.

Lisa liked this dance because she got to hold his beautiful hand through the entire song, never once changing partners, never once letting go of him, never once losing sight of him. She felt like she was walking on air the whole time. Even though the music was simple and rustic, with the stars and the night sky, she felt like she was in paradise. She didn't want it to end. But it did. The dance ended as quietly as it started and harvest fest was over. He kissed her hand then disappeared.

Lisa had turned to talk to a gaggle of giggling girls that wanted to be introduced to her dance partner. When Lisa turned back to Giuliano to accommodate them, he was no longer there. He and his friends had vanished into the night. It would be a long time before she would see him again.

Chapter 18 – Signore Rucellai

The Gherardini family, mother and father, and their eight children, including Lisa, returned to Florence the following day. The harvest had not been a good one. Antonmaria was worried about the future.

Lisa was in ninth heaven, her mind filled with memories of her time with her lover – lying with Giuliano in the field of flowers; Giuliano with the flaming brand protecting her from the wolves; dancing the night away holding Giuliano's hand. She went through the days with a luster in her eyes, and that hint of a smile she would one day be known for.

Caterina knew why but kept it to herself. Lisa's secret would not be allowed to interfere with their plans.

"We must marry Lisa off," said Caterina to her husband. "The harvest was not as good as we had wished for. We do not have enough to buy seed for next year and survive the winter. Lisa is our only hope."

"I know. I will see what I can do," Anton replied. "I was hoping the young gentleman she met at the harvest dance would stay around. I never got to meet him. Perhaps …"

"It is of no use, Anton," Caterina informed him. "He was just a passing fancy. Nothing will become of it, but I have a few things we can try."

Lisa's father took the opportunity to talk to his daughter and reaffirm her duty to her family. She nodded appropriately but did not seem committed one way or another. It did not matter. She would get married, or they would perish.

The days tumbled into weeks, which slid into months. Lisa did not see Giuliano for all this time. Christmas passed and then the New Year. The memory of his face was fading. The recollection of his touch had gone. She was left with emptiness and heartache.

"Oh, dear God," she lamented one night to the heavens. "When will I see him again? I long for him so. Please give me a sign. Is my lover safe? Is he of good health? Does he long for me as I do for him? Oh, that I could only see him again."

Her joy had turned to tears, her happiness to loneliness.

Just when it seemed things could be no more desperate, her mother called her down one morning with news. She was to meet a suitor.

"He is a third cousin of my father's," said her stepmother. "He is well-off and looking for a new wife. His third one just passed away. He is an older gentleman and most of his children are grown up, but he still has a few little ones to care for, as well as a newborn his late wife brought into the world before she passed. He is eager to meet you. His carriage is coming for you this afternoon at the seventh hour. Maria will go with you."

"So soon," Lisa answered. "I will not have time to get ready."

"Do not worry. You will be fine. I will help you wash your hair so that it looks nice and silky for him. It is one of your most striking features, that along with your dark eyes and full lips."

"How old is your cousin?" asked Lisa.

"It does not matter. He is in good physical shape."

"Of course it matters," objected Lisa. "If I am to marry someone, I should at least know how old the person is."

"He is fifty-six but looks much younger."

"Fifty-six! Oh, Mamma, must I?"

"Yes, you must. Did not your father explain how important this is for our family? You must do your duty."

"Duty, duty! That is all I hear. What about me? Do I not have any say in this?"

"We are lucky there are still some who are interested in you after what happened with those dreadful Medici. You are lucky your name has not been completely ruined only tattered."

"Giuliano still loves me!" Lisa shouted.

Her stepmother struck her sharply across the face. The slap sounded like a whip cracking. Lisa was more surprised than hurt, but held her cheek anyway.

"We will sell you to the gypsies if you defy us in this matter," her stepmother threatened. "Now get ready."

Lisa did as she was told. She had already resigned herself to her fate, despite the momentary rebellion.

The suitor's carriage arrived as expected and whisked Lisa and her chaperone away across town, to another part of the city. Lisa sat as if made of stone, staring straight ahead the whole way. She kept her mind a blank, hardly noticing her surroundings as she passed through the center of Florence, her thoughts dark and melancholy. Maria, who sat next to her in the back of the carriage, hardly noticed her charge's mood, and chattered on to no one in particular about all she saw.

They stopped at a palatial villa just inside the western wall. It sat on a rise and had a magnificent view of that part of the city. Like most of the large villas in the area, it was surrounded by gardens and tall trees.

Signore Rucellai was a stout man with large shoulders and wide hips. The hair he had left was gray and ringed his pallet leaving most of it hairless. His eyes were watery and faded-gray, as if the color had been drained out of them with age.

He looked her up and down greedily. It appeared to Lisa like he was drooling. His lips were wet, his chin moist with spittle.

He showed her the house, which was filled with rich furniture and heirlooms, and the grounds, which were covered with shrubs and rose bushes. His children, at least those still living with him, were also introduced - a boy of twelve, two girls, seven and three, and a three-month-old baby boy.

In spite of her trepidation, Lisa spent a long time playing with the little boy, which gratified the old man greatly. Things went well until he took her into the library alone. He did not take her there to read. Maria, who had already been cowered by Signore Rucellai's glare and wealth, said nothing as she was left alone in the vestibule.

Closing the door behind him, he said, "Undress."

It was said as an order, as if he was used to people jumping at his command. Lisa did not move.

"I am sorry," she said. "What did you say?"

"I said undress," he repeated. "Take your dress off and your blouse."

"I will do no such thing," she answered. "I will only undress in front of my husband."

"How can I decide if I want to marry you or not, if I do not see what you look like?"

"You can see well enough what I look like. I am as I am. I have two arms and two legs, a nose and a mouth, two eyes and ears. What do you have to see that you cannot see now, that I have to take my clothes off?"

"I need to see that you are a chaste woman," the old man said.

"You, sir, are a cad!" she replied. "My mother, your cousin, has vouched for my chastity. Are you calling her a liar? She will not take kindly to that."

"Do not play coy with me, child. I know all about you. I need to see if you can birth babies or not. Now take your clothes off."

As he said these words, he took her by the arm and pulled her toward him. Then he lifted her smock above her waist and pinched her on the behind, taking a good inch of skin in his fingers.

"Ouch!" Lisa yelled, slapping his hand and pulling the dress back down. "Stop that. It is very rude, Signore."

"Ha ha," he laughed. "I see you are a playful wench. You have some spunk. I like that."

"I am no wench at all, Signore."

He reached for her again, but she darted away and ran past him to the door.

"Come back here!" he yelled as she ran out of the room toward the exit.

The old man chased after her, shouting to his servants.

"Stop her! Stop her!"

They all scurried to do his bidding. Maria, who was still sitting in the hallway, stood and gaped in horror as pandemonium took place around her.

One of the servants grabbed Lisa from behind, pinning her arms. She stomped on his foot and bit his hand, breaking away. Another tried to block her path as she ran toward the front door. She ran into him at full speed, pushing him aside and knocking him down. Then she was out of the building running down the long drive.

There she stood panting as Maria came jogging down the road screaming hysterically. They ran blindly for several blocks, totally disoriented, and ended up lost.

They were not that far from home, but Lisa knew she would not be able to navigate their way through the maze of narrow streets and side alleys to her villa. To make matters worse, it would be dark soon.

Not knowing what else to do, they followed the wall as it circled the town. Her family's villa was not far from the wall. They hoped to eventually arrive at a part of it that they recognized. In this way, they eventually found their way home, but only after walking two-thirds of the circumference of Florence.

It was late at night by the time they arrived, three hours later, exhausted and famished. Lisa's parents were both up waiting for her. Maria, shocked and still hysterical, tried but could not explain what had occurred. Her tongue was tied and her thoughts were scattered.

"What happened?" her stepmother asked Lisa finally.

"We have been worried sick about you," said her father.

"We thought you would be back hours ago, but Rucellai's coach never returned," added his wife.

"It was horrible," sobbed Lisa. "What a horrible man. He tried to take my clothes off! He pinched me!"

"He did not have a female relative there to examine you?" asked her father.

"This was supposed to be an initial meeting only," her stepmother explained. "The examination was to come later. Uncle Julius is a little headstrong at times. You must not take it amiss, Lisa."

"I will not go back there," Lisa told them. "He is a terrible man."

"I will talk to your cousin," said Anton angrily to his wife. "If this is true ..."

It soon became a moot point. Signore Rucellai's carriage came by that morning with a messenger. The note he delivered said that the gentleman was no longer interested in Signora Gherardini. Furthermore, the gentleman promised to let all his acquaintances and family know that the Gherardini girl is an unchaste, belligerent, ignorant puttana.

As if things were not bad enough for Lisa and her family, this had to happen. Anton was crushed. Caterina, angry and disappointed, was more determined than ever to find a suitor for her daughter.

Chapter 19 – Bartolommeo Bonachelli

Antonmarie came home excited one evening a few days after the disastrous affair with signore Rucellai.

"I found a suitor," he said. "His name is Bartolommeo and he is only a couple of years older than you, Lisa. He is a big boy and not bad to look at. His father is a landowner in St. Donado, just like us. His son saw Lisa dancing at the festival and told him he wanted to marry her. His mother objects but I promised Signore Bonachelli the farm as a dowry, so he is willing to concede to his only son's wishes."

"That is wonderful news, is it not, Lisa?" gushed Caterina. "We must meet this Bartolommeo."

"He is expecting us this afternoon," Anton told them.

Lisa said nothing.

"Ah, that is excellent." said her stepmother.

Lisa remained silent as her father drove the twenty miles to St. Donato, where they were to meet the suitor. Her brothers and sisters were in the back of the wagon and would form the majority of chaperones, along with their father. Lisa would not be alone this time.

She was dressed in a heavy, pleated smock over a simple white blouse. The blouse was modestly low-cut, and showed a good deal of Lisa's neck and collar bone. Her hair was in a thin veil, which was barely visible above her long, dark-brown trusses.

While her mouth was silent, her mind was abuzz with thoughts and doubts At least the suitor was her age and had no deformities, if she could believe her father's description. Surely, he would not lie to her about that. Or would he? If he was desperate enough? Unfortunately, she knew that he was. She would know the truth soon enough.

How far was she willing to go for her family? Did she even have a choice? She became aware that her father had said something to her.

"Try not to offend him right off," he advised her. "Give him a chance. He is not such a bad lad and a hard worker too. He will do well with San Silvestro."

"You are giving him our farm?" she said in surprise.

"But of course," answered her father as if the question was absurd. "It is your dowry. How else do you think we could have gotten you married?"

"You treat me like a cow you bring to market," she observed.

"That is not true. We treat you like any first-born female child."

"Yes, like chattel. It is barbaric."

"Lisa, where do you learn such words?"

"I read."

"What, those dirty romance novels? It is barely intelligible dribble. It has ruined your mind. That is why you must do as your parents say so as to not fall into destructive error."

"I will do as you say, Papa. I would not want to disappoint you for all you are doing for me. I want to help our family."

She vaguely remembered who Bartolommeo was. She had seen him around. He was a big, quiet boy with a bowl-haircut and long arms. She had seen him on the streets of the village and at the church with his family, as well as at the annual harvest festivals, where he usually sat alone. She had never even had eye contact with him, let alone spoken to him. She would speak to him this day, however.

Arriving at the Bonachelli farm, Lisa and her father got out of the wagon. Signore Bonachelli met them at the threshold of his home and invited them in for refreshments, buttermilk for the children, Chianti for the adults. Then Bartolommeo and Lisa walked along the dusty road that ran through his father's property. Lisa's father walked several feet behind them with Lisa's siblings tagging along at their own pace.

The first things she noticed about Bartolommeo were that his fingernails were encrusted with black dirt and he had terrible body order. Not only that, his breath and hands smelled like raw onions, which he had obviously eaten recently.

He was dull-eyed and mumbled an awkward greeting when introduced. He was large. Everything about him was big – his head, his body, his hands, his feet. He must have stood six feet, a giant compared with the average five and a half foot Italian. His boot size must have measured thirty centimeters.

They walked for some time before one of them spoke.

"You dance really good," he said. "I saw you at the festival."

"Thank you. Were you there? I did not see you."

"That is because you danced with that dandy all night."

"Oh, yes, he was from the university or something, on his way to Verona."

"Good riddance, the fancy pants," said Bartolommeo.

There was another lapse in the conversation. Lisa could not believe how ridiculous the situation was. Even though Bartolommeo was two years older than her, he seemed to be more like her little brother, Nolto, in age.

What was she doing here? Did her parents really expect her to marry this oaf? Then she remembered what she had promised her father and resolved to give the boy a chance.

"You are very pretty." Bartolommeo said.

"You are too kind, sir," she replied.

"My mother said you are a ruined woman, for having a dalliance with a prince."

"That is not true," Lisa objected. "Your mother is mistaken, Signore."

"She is not, but I don't care. I want to marry you anyway. You are pretty. You dance nice."

Lisa said nothing, but stopped walking. Bartolommeo stopped as well.

"I want to marry you also, kind Signore, but I am sworn to marry only a military man, for my honor. For if not, I will die of shame by my own hand, on my own funeral bier. It is my pledge."

She began walking again. She had not planned the words. They had come to her spontaneously of their own accord. The effect was instantaneous, however. Her suitor stood motionless behind her. She ignored him and kept walking. He ran up to her breathlessly and confused.

"No one said anything about the military. I am a farmer, not a soldier."

"No one consulted me either," she replied. "Now that we are together discussing our future, I can tell you. If you want me, you must defend my honor for a year with the city defense or the duke's levies. The French and Spanish are at our gates. Who will defend me, dear sir? Will you throw me to the heathens? I beg of you, Signore. Defend my honor and I will be your loving wife and dance for you at dinner."

She stopped and raised her arm in the air dramatically.

"I will take my life here and now, and plunge a dagger into my heart, if I am to marry without my honor."

At this point her arm came down as if to plunge a knife into her heart.

"Please, Signore, save me or I must die."

Lisa's pretended ardor touched the young man's heart. He was fired with her cause. If she would surrender herself and dance for him, he would brave any danger. If she would be his wife, he would risk death itself.

"I will have to talk to father," said the youth. "He will know what to do."

"No!" answered Lisa, thinking fast. "Tell no one. They will only try to dissuade you. Just say to them the time is not right. Then do what you must. I will be waiting."

The walk was terminated abruptly. No reason was given, to the consternation of everyone involved. Anton and his brood left soon after, without spending the night.

"What did you say?" Lisa's father asked her.

"I don't think he wants to marry me," she replied.

"Why? What did you do?"

"Nothing. He decided he is not ready to get married. He has things he wants to do first."

"What? How could he change his mind like that? What did you say to him?"

"Nothing, Papa. Perhaps he realized he was not ready for marriage and all the responsibility it entails. You should be happy, Papa. You will not have to give our farm away as a dowry."

"Oh, dear Lord, what are we to do with you?" cried Anton. "What will become of us with a first-born such as this?"

Chapter 20 – Giuliano's Request

Giuliano was in constant motion, moving through the city between the Medici villa and the seat of government, the Pallazzo della Signoria. He was diligent in his duties with the city council, where he looked out for his older brother's interests.

Despite all this activity, his mind was forever on his Lisa. The scent of her hair – he could still smell it on the handkerchief she gave him; the feel of her body when he pressed against her – he became aroused just thinking of it; the taste of her lips – so sweet and soft.

The thought of her made the blood in his temples pulse – and other places as well. He desired her more than all things, even air and water. He would almost rather not breathe than be without her. The thought that he might see her again made things tolerable. He would persist and keep going through each day as long as there was that hope.

He was doing as his brother Piero had asked. Working for the family and the city – they were practically inseparable now – to keep the inhabitants safe and prosperous. That was the task of the ruler, and that is what he and his brother were – rulers of Florence.

The position came with privileges and responsibilities, both great.

"The Council is turning against us," Giuliano informed his brother Piero for the tenth time that month. "They say your treaty negotiators are giving away too much."

"What would they have me do?" responded his older brother, their father, Lorenzo's heir. "France is like a hungry wolf ready to strike. He wants Pisa. We do not have a weapon strong enough to stop him. We must feed him to keep him docile and contented so that we may, in time, train and tame him."

"Yes, and in the meantime it is the council that will devour you. You cannot rule without them."

"I know, Giuliano, I know," answered Piero. "Oh, that father had not died."

"I want to see Lisa," said Giuliano out of the blue.

He had not mentioned her name for many months. Giovanni was in Rome at the Vatican. Uncle Giuliano was in Naples. Lisa's lover had lost his conduit to her. He had no way of getting word to her or information about her, and it was driving him mad.

"What?" said Piero, both annoyed and shocked.

"I must know how she is," said Giuliano, "if she is all right or not. I want to see to her future, since I am responsible for her misfortune and suffering, through no fault of her own."

"No, Giuliano, that is out of the question," replied his brother. "You know better than to ask that. We are undertaking sensitive discussions with King Charles in France over Pisa. There are also troubles between Ferranty of Naples and Sforza in Milan. Now is a delicate time. Our cities fight among themselves, while the real enemy, the French, grow strong. They would all use your relationship with that girl to our disadvantage."

"No one will know," replied Giuliano. "I will work secretly behind the scenes to aid her, but I must see her again so that she understands and goes along. Otherwise, everything will be for naught and she and her family will be destroyed. It is for the grace of God that I ask this."

Piero was silent for a moment as he considered his younger brother's words.

"She is not your concern, Giuliano," he finally answered. "You will have greater things to worry about soon with the French if we are not careful."

Giuliano looked at his older brother, by seven years, long and hard. Even though he was their father's heir, Piero was not the smartest Medici in the house, just the opposite. He had little sense of discipline, yet acted as if he were the hero of a Greek drama. Arrogant and feeble, he made a poor ruler as would soon be seen.

"In any case," stated Piero. "The pre-Lenten carnival will soon be here. You will be able to carry on with any number of lusty wenches. As a matter of fact, I have business in Pisa. I want you to join me. There is someone there I want you to meet. She will make you forget all about your precious Lisa."

Chapter 21 – Lucrezia

Giuliano was not interested in meeting anyone but went along with his brother's suggestion out of sheer boredom, anything to get out of the city where he was suffocating without his love. The aching in his heart was unbearable, knowing she was so near and yet not being able to see her. They traveled to Pisa, where Piero was to meet with the French envoys, and the young maiden was waiting.

"She is fourteen and very pretty," Piero told him. "She was married to the lord of Pesaro recently, but that marriage was annulled by Papal decree."

"Oh, she must come from a powerful family," observed Giuliano.

"Si, she is related to the Borgia pope."

"You have mentioned that name before."

"Her name is Lucrezia," his brother informed him.

A short time later they entered Pisa and found lodging at the ducal palace, where the young lady was staying as well. They all supped together. Then Piero left to meet with the French envoys, who were there at their King's command. Charles claimed Pisa as his rightful inheritance, while Florence asserted it was theirs. Giuliano and the young Borgia girl were left alone together, as Piero had planned.

"My brother speaks very highly of you," Giuliano told her, opening up the conversation.

"He seems nice. He has high hopes for your city," said Lucrezia.

"Yes, he is a very diligent ruler and doing his best to manage things with the French."

She was slender, with long, golden hair that went down to the floor. Her face was like an angel's, perfectly symmetrical with flawless skin. She moved with grace and spoke well. Obviously intelligent, she had held up her end of the conversation with the guests at supper exceedingly well.

She wore a long, colorful gown with a modest neckline and gossamer sleeves, together with a sheer, shimmering robe. A pearl necklace graced her neck. A ring with a precious green stone was on her left third finger.

Her smile was stunning. She had been flashing it at Giuliano all night. Now she was studying him closely.

"Are you a good kisser?" she asked suddenly.

Giuliano wasn't sure he had heard her correctly.

"What?" he stammered.

"Never mind," she said. "I will find out for myself."

With that, she leaned forward and kissed him on the lips. Giuliano did nothing at first, but then realizing he was being tested as a man, he returned the kiss. They held it long and it became more passionate as the moments passed. Finally, she let up and sighed.

"It is important to me that my men be good kissers," she told him. "You will do."

"You take much for granted, don't you," Giuliano replied.

"I know what I want. Why should only men have that privilege?"

"Because we earned it," he answered.

"Would you like to kiss my bosoms? I am told they are very pretty."

"By whom? Do you allow anyone to do so?"

"Only those that strike my fancy."

She felt his biceps and looked him up and down.

"You have big feet. That is a good sign."

He did not like being measured like a hunk of beef, especially by someone so young.

"You are quite precocious for one your age."

"It is how I was brought up."

"I would say you were not brought up very well."

"I would say you are rude," she replied. "One could say the same of you."

"Now I know why you were not married long."

"I, like you, am a pawn to be moved about as those above me wish. I had no say in the marriage – I was only thirteen – and no say in the annulment. It is all the same to me."

"It has made you hard," he observed. "Girls should be soft. Then one would want to kiss their bosoms."

"You can kiss my arse, Signore."

Giuliano burst out laughing. "You certainly are an entertaining girl."

"I am happy I made you laugh. Laughter can cure all ills," she said.

"Si, to laugh is good. One would be laughing all the time with you, I'll wager."

"Thank you. I take that as a compliment, for I was trying to make you laugh and I succeeded."

"That you did. May I call you Lucrezia?" he asked.

"Yes, please do and I will call you Signore Giuliano, a good Italian name."

"I am glad that you like it."

"Why are you not talking to the French envoys like your brother?" she asked. "Are you not ruler of Florence?"

"My older brother, Piero, was my father's heir."

"And how does your father's heir treat you? Why do you not accompany him on state business? It appears he treats you like a child."

"That is not so. I help him govern the city, but he wanted me to meet you. That is why I am here. Otherwise, I would be back in Florence taking care of things for him."

"I see. You, like me, are a pawn for others to manipulate. Be careful he does not sacrifice you."

"I am my own man," insisted Giuliano, even though he knew it was not true. Otherwise he would be with his Lisa now, and not this vamp.

"Sure you are, little brother," she answered laughing. "If you are not ruler of Florence, why am I wasting my time with you?"

"If you think I am a waste of time, my lady, I will be happy to take my leave."

"No, please, I find you entertaining as well. Besides, you are more comely than your older brother and I'll wager smarter, but he is not good to you."

"How do you know? You know nothing about us."

"Ah, that is not so. I have heard all about you. How you have ruined a young girl's name with your dalliance."

Giuliano was stunned to silence to learn that she had heard about this.

Beet red with embarrassment, he finally spoke.

"That is not true. It is rumor only, but that is bad enough. She is a chaste girl, unlike you, and has done nothing wrong. We love each other but are not allowed to meet due to my father's ban."

"Love you say? What is that? You feel for her like you do for a small kitten or your horse?"

"You know nothing of love and you never will. I feel sorry for you."

"Spare me, Signore. I find you tiresome."

"You are not a nice girl," he said. "One does not know how to take you. Is everything a joke to you? Or are you really so cynical that nothing means anything to you?"

76

"You should take me seriously, Signore," she replied, her eyes flashing. "For my family is very powerful and we will do anything and use anyone to get what we want."

"And what do you want?" he asked.

"I do not know, but it is not you."

With that she left him standing alone.

"Ah, that is a good thing, I think," Giuliano replied to the empty room.

Chapter 22 – Carnival

Lisa's father became concerned when he had not heard from Signore Bonachelli for several days concerning his son's intentions. He was thinking of taking the wagon and driving to the Bonachelli villa, when word from them arrived by messenger. Bonachelli's son, Bartolommeo, had run away and joined the duke's levies guarding the borders against French incursions.

Senore Bonachelli thanked Antonmaria for considering their son a suitor for their daughter and told him to thank his daughter for the lace veil she had left his son as a token of her affection.

Anton looked at his daughter questioningly when he heard this, but she feigned innocence. She tried not to smile, but was elated that her little spur-of-the-moment ploy had actually worked. She just hoped the poor boy would not be hurt. She would deal with him in a year. That is, if he survived that long.

It was carnival time again. She had not heard from Giuliano since the harvest dance. Did he still love her? Had he forgotten about her? It must be harder to send her messages here in the city, but she was hurt he had not tried. Perhaps there was something wrong. He had been hurt or was sick. Why had he not contacted her?

She was sick at heart. Discouraged with how things were going. She dreaded another suitor from her parents, who were scraping the bottom of the barrel as far as she was concerned. Her life had become a sour stream of nauseous days. Carnival was a beam of light in the darkness, floating closer with the passing days. If only her little bark could make it before it sank.

The week of carnival was finally upon them, but she felt no joy. Everyone around her was gay and happy, busy preparing, making costumes, planning parties, but her heart felt like lead. She pretended to be jolly but she was not a very good actor.

"What is wrong, Lisa? Things cannot be as bad as all that," said her stepmother. "Your father will find another suitor."

"That is what I am afraid of," Lisa answered. "I will die before I marry such as you have brought me."

"Oh, Lisa, do not be so melodramatic. It does not become you. Be gay. Make yourself attractive so that you will attract a man. We will make you an alluring costume. Would you like to be a dancing girl?"

"Make me a corpse, covered with blood," Lisa replied. "Make me a devil dressed in red."

"Goodness, Lisa, you will not attract anyone like that. Do you want to be the ruin of us?"

"Why do you not just sell me in the market like a piece of meat? That is all I am to you."

"It is for you that we do this," said her stepmother. "Do you not want to be happy and have a good life? Do you not want a family and your own household? A good marriage is one of the great blessings of heaven. I found it with Anton. You will find it with someone. Just trust in God. It is a sin to shirk a family duty."

"I will become a nun then, and dedicate myself to the church."

"That will help no one. Anyway, I know you, Lisa, you would not like the convent. Why do you want to punish yourself?"

"Because I cannot have Giuliano. If I cannot have him, I want no one. There is no life without him."

"There is plenty of life without that cad and his family. You mark my words. There will come a day when they will not be riding so high and mighty. Their days are numbered."

"Do not say that," cried Lisa. "That is a terrible thing to say."

"Then forget about him," advised her stepmother. "Go to the carnival with the others and find another."

The day of the carnival arrived. Lisa spent her time alone in a back shed making her costume. The full-face, papier-mâché mask was painted all white with the black facial features of a crying clown. Black painted tears dripped from the eyes. The costume was a black burial shroud.

No one had seen it. She kept it hidden and told none. If she felt no joy, she would exude suffering and pain.

None of her family saw her leave the villa. She left alone. Revelers in devil costumes ran riotously down the streets. People drank to excess. Drunken men caroused on the street corners and sang bawdy songs. Couples groped and grabbed each other in dark alleys, while licentious old men chased young women in broad daylight. Lisa walked silently through it all.

The Duomo Piazza was mobbed. The Pallazzo swarmed with partiers. Merchants and artisans, tailors and money lenders, silk weavers and wood carvers, clerics and stone cutters, men, women, everyone was out on the streets. People had come from hundreds of miles. The costumed cavorted and danced, bought and sold, laughed and clapped, yelled and stamped, but Lisa noticed none of it. She was searching for Giuliano.

He had to be here, somewhere. Would she recognize him? Was he masked?

She circled the Piazza searching. The Medici heraldic crest floated above the crowds, held up on banners and street posts. Lavishly decorated floats rolled by, pulled by oxen, horses, and men, depicting great battle scenes and Greek myths. Team battled team in triumphs and jousts. Passion plays and crude farces entertained the populace, along with jugglers and acrobats.

Lisa hunted the throng for that familiar frame, the dark, curly hair and those muscular legs. She looked every male over boldly, not being deterred by their stares. Even during carnival, where unusual behavior was the norm, Lisa stood out as odd. She was on a quest.

She called his name several times, when she came upon one who resembled her lover in some guise or disguise. Some even answered to the name. None was the Medici, however.

Finally giving up, she circled the plaza, seeking a quiet place of solitude. She soon found one, the grotto beneath the Loggia della Signoria, where she and Giuliano first kissed each other.

Even the noise of carnival was blocked out by the thick stone walls and ceiling. She sat on the bench beneath the arch. Closing her eyes, she began to cry, her real tears staining the painted ones of her mask.

Giuliano, back in Florence, bided his time. He knew that his brother had no discipline and would be celebrating hard during carnival. Piero would most likely be lying besotted in some gutter or a strange bed. Giuliano did not even bother wearing a costume, but walked the streets without a mask. After his encounter with the Borgia girl, he had longed for Lisa's fresh and honest nature even more.

He'd had no word from her, no indication of whether she was alive or dead, or where she might be. He had walked to her home and watched from across the street each day of Carnival, but she had not appeared. Then, when he saw someone leave the villa with the bizarre mask of sorrow, wearing a shroud, he knew immediately that it was her. He followed quietly behind.

He knew she was looking for him, but he did not dare show himself among so many people. Any one of them could have been

80

Piero or a friend. Despite his urge to show himself and ease her suffering, he did nothing. When he saw her go into the Loggia, his heart leapt for joy. It was just what he had hoped she would do.

Walking down the wide stone steps, he approached her quietly.

"Lisa, my love, I am here," he said.

Lisa was so overwhelmed by his sudden appearance that she swooned when she stood up too abruptly. Giuliano caught her as she stumbled and nearly fell. Taking her in his arms, he laid her on a bench in a dark, secluded corner, and stood over her. Taking off her sorrowful masked, he bathed her tearful face with kisses.

"Oh, my Lisa. I am so sorry I have been away from you so long. I have thought of you every minute of every day, wondering when I would see you again. The affairs of state and my brother have kept me away. I have missed you so. I knew you would come here. I followed you but could not reveal myself until we were alone."

"Giuliano, is it you, my dearest? I could not hope to meet you, but here you are. I have waited so long that I thought it would never happen. My prayers have been answered."

As she said this, he kissed her passionately on the mouth, so hard and long that she could not breathe. His hands were all over her, almost ripping the thin costume from her body. He kissed her everywhere he touched her - her neck, her shoulder, her stomach, her breasts, her pelvis, her legs. No inch of her was not touched and kissed.

She did the same to him, exploring him for the first time, everything, shamelessly. The feel of his flesh, his muscles and bones, gave her great pleasure. They soon had their clothes off. Naked, they both bathed in the beauty of the other.

What happened that night exceeded all their expectations and filled them with such joy and love that the tender images and memories would last for the rest of their lives.

Chapter 23 – A Year Passes

The year 1493 passed peacefully and uneventfully for Lisa and her family. The memory of that magical carnival night stayed with her through the days and months that followed. It was reinforced by occasional nocturnal visits. She was given more leeway and independence when she turned another year older in June, though she still had her chores to do and continued to be chaperoned.

Although she and Giuliano had been intimate and lied together naked, she was still a virgin. They had done everything you could do short of actual intercourse.

There had been no more talk of suitors. A good harvest would help see to that, though her parents were still worried that she would end up an old maid. To still these worries, she told them what Giuliano had said when they last parted.

"He told me even though he could not marry me, he did not want me to be hurt by his actions. He promised to see that I would have a proper suitor."

"How is he to do this?" asked Caterina. "Are we to have no say in the matter?"

"No, he will work with you and Papa to make it happen," Lisa explained. "He said to trust him."

"Humph!" snorted her stepmother. "We can trust him to ruin our name well enough."

"No, Caterina, I think we can trust Signore Medici," Antonmaria said. "He has many more connections than we have. Let us be patient and see. Even though Lisa has had another birthday, she is still young."

"Si, but she will not stay so," replied his wife.

Giuliano, the same age as Lisa, had also grown. He was an important man now, a prominent figure in the Signoria. Many thought more of him than they did his older, simpler brother, Piero. His other brother, Giovanni, was also maturing, rising in the church hierarchy through his learning and astuteness.

A dull listlessness had descended upon the world, at least that part of it that Giuliano lived in. Or was it just him? The days were long and hot, the nights damp and humid. Things went along of their own accord, with no one paying much attention.

Giuliano often daydreamed about Lisa. Not one of the girls who might be likely spouses for him could be considered desirable. They were all either too young, or too old, or just plain too ugly. Especially unappealing was the young Borgia girl who had acted so shamefully. Or was it just an act, to discourage him perhaps?

He wanted Lisa more than ever. No one else would do. He was forever hatching schemes to have her, including running away and stealing the Medici art treasures to sell for gold coin. Still, he bided his time, watching and waiting. He made himself useful in the meantime.

"Congratulations on the treaty negotiations," he said to Piero as they supped. "They went well, I hear."

"Si, we are lucky. Ferranty in Naples and Sforza in Milan are getting along, at least for the time being. It is one less thing to worry about. I hear the Duke of Savoy is looking for a suitor for his daughter."

"She is but nine or ten," Giuliano objected.

"She is old enough," his brother responded. "In any case, she is not that much younger than you."

"She is but a child," answered the younger Medici.

"Yes, and you are an old man, not yet twenty. It is all relative, I suppose."

It was the end of a hot, late September day. Giuliano had not mentioned Lisa to Piero since Carnival, several months before. It appeared that he had forgotten her as Piero had wished. So when he asked his older brother if he could take the carriage to the country with some friends for the evening, Piero had no objections.

Giuliano had become quite discreet in his dealings, both private and public. He had a servant visit the Gherardini villa, where he learned Lisa was there alone. It was harvest time and the family had left for the country. She had stayed back to lock up the house. She would follow in a few days with more furniture and provisions in the wagon.

The messenger told her that Giuliano would be by early that evening to pick her up.

He arrived just before sunset in a nondescript carriage. Leaving the city walls, he took her out to the hills overlooking Florence. Stopping at a clearing on the western slope, they looked out at the stunning view. No one else was there. The soft wind and evening bird songs were the only sounds. A hush had come over the world as if a blanket of peace was being laid over it, as if God had blinked his eyes shut for a moment's rest from all His cares.

They sat on the soft grass watching the sun sink slowly behind the distant mountains. The whole sky lay open before them. The colors changed like a slowly rotating kaleidoscope – yellow, gold, red, purple, white, and finally black and moonlight.

All that time, while the horizon changed from hue to hue, they clung to each other. And when it was over they kissed and cried for the sheer beauty of it. Lisa remained a virgin, but perhaps no longer so chaste.

They slept together under the moon, spending the night beneath the stars. He took her home before the sun was up. No one noticed. No one saw. Her parents trusted her. They had no choice. She showed up at the farm the next afternoon and life went on as before.

Giuliano had never come so close to intercourse. He was afraid he may have gone too far. What if she became pregnant? That would be a mistake for all. Then again, it might be the best thing that could happen.

He would take her away, perhaps to France, and live happily ever after. He would take some of the artwork to sell. She would no longer have an excuse to say no. Her family would not be able to object. They would have to do the best they could without her. The more he thought of it, the better the idea seemed. He began to form a concrete plan in his mind.

He vowed that he would get her pregnant and take her away with him.

Chapter 24 – Buon Anno 1494

The sky lit up in bright red and yellow brilliance as fireworks burst in the air. Loud explosions jarred the night. Lisa and her siblings followed the crowd of spectators into the Cathedral square. It was the Feast of the Epiphany. As during carnival many of the crowd was masked, but there was none of the drinking and licentiousness as at the pre-Lenten season.

It would be easy to lose her brothers and sisters. Giovangual was with his friends and not there. The little ones were older now and the next oldest, Ginevera and Berto were watching them. Lisa would not be missed.

She had received word from Giuliano earlier that day by secret message, dropped under a stone by the well in front of her villa. The note said to meet him at their rendezvous place under the Loggia della Signoria.

For some reason she was reluctant to go. She could not have told you why. Some inner foreboding, a subtle hint that something was not quite right nagged at her. She should have been giddy with the prospect of seeing her lover again, but she was afraid. All her senses were on alert, ready to flee at any moment.

Giuliano was there waiting for her. He came out of a dark corner when he heard her come down the stone steps.

"I have been waiting," he told her. "I have something for you."

He showed her a wooden board with cat-gut strings strung in a narrow, parallel band across the top. In the other hand he held a bow.

"I have been studying the lyre these past few months with Atalante Migliorotti, a student of the Master. My father sent the great maestro to Milan, where he now works for Duke Lodovico Sforza."

"I have heard you speak of him and of the Duke," said Lisa. "I hear the Duke is a very great man, but tell me more about this master you speak of."

"Leonardo? Ah, he is a master of so many things. He is a painter divine, as well as a military engineer and sculptor. He now, as we speak, is designing what will be the largest, most fantastic bronze equestrian statue ever made. It will be one of the wonders of the world some day."

"I would like to meet this maestro you speak so highly of," she said.

"Who knows?" Giuliano replied. "Maybe one day he will paint your picture."

He bowed the lyre, making the strings sing in sweet harmony. Then he began to sing.

Your love - - - grips my heart ---
Like hoops of steel ---,
Memories --- of you ---
Are so rich and real----,
Your image --- haunts me
When we part---,
When we --- are --- together ---
You fill--- my --- heart ---

She listened transfixed like a mouse before a cat. She could hardly hear the words through the beating of her heart. It was a love song. Of that she was sure. There was nothing to fear. Why was she so afraid? She was trembling.

He put down the lyre and the bow and held her. Playing her like the instrument, his hands glided over her, touching her in the most intimate places. He removed her garments ever so gently, like plucking the petals from a rose.

"You are so beautiful," he whispered as he caressed her. "Ti amore. You are everything to me – il sole, la luna, le stelle. They are dim without you, without your eyes, without your lips, without your smile. I am nothing without you. I need you so. Sii il mio amore fino alla fine dei tempi."

Dropping his rose-colored hose, he stood half-naked and erect before her. She could do nothing but stare. It was beautiful and hideous at the same time, threatening and pacifying. She hardly breathed as he moved to her and held her, kissing her.

She guided him toward her. "No," she breathed, hardly audible.

Just then the sound of someone coming down the steps interrupted their love-making.

"Who is there?" said the voice. "What are you doing here?"

"It is I, Giuliano de Medici. What do you want?" he announced, quickly pulling his tights on.

"Oh, it is you. Sorry, Signore. There have been reports of vandalism. I just came down to investigate."

"Si, I have heard the same. That is why I am here. It looks like I beat you to it. Everything is as it should be. I will be up soon. You can go."

"Si, Signore, grazie. Buon anno."

When Giuliano went back to where Lisa had been, she was no longer there. She had crept past him while he and the intruder talked. She ran out of the Loggia and did not stop until she was home, not sure what had or had not happened.

Chapter 25 – The Visit

Several months passed. Giuliani had sent secret messages to Lisa many times, but none of them were answered. When the messenger went to leave a note, the preceding one was still there. Lisa answered none of them. She knew what would happen if she did.

She was torn between her lover and her family. She knew that if she saw Giuliano again he would take her totally. If he did, she would likely be with child soon after. She had seen it happen enough times. It would surely be the ruin of her and her family. She would have to run away with him.

She was tempted, but every time she looked at her father and siblings, that temptation grew less urgent. She had promised them. Giuliano had promised to take care of her. Is that what he meant? Had he changed his mind? Had he gone back on his word to help her? She thought he loved her, now she wasn't sure. Maybe he wanted her, and love had nothing to do with it.

Lisa wanted him, too, but she wanted to be his wife. If she could not be his spouse, then she would marry another, if possible, someone who would help her family. She would be a chaste bride, but she would choose the suitor. She would not have demented old men and ignorant, uncouth boys.

She was another year older. She had told no one about the recent incident or her fears. She read none of Giuliano's letters. Still, she had to know the truth, one way or another. She could not live in perpetual uncertainty. She had to see him, but on her own terms.

She had long since learned where he lived. It was not a very long walk once you knew the way. She had even viewed the villa one evening, but had not seen anyone. She decided to visit it again and confront Giuliano.

She left her home early before the sun was up. She wanted to get there to catch him before he left for the Signoria. No one saw her leave, which was not unusual. She could not be watched at all hours of the day and night. Furthermore, she and Maria had an understanding, which they each benefitted from. What her parents didn't know, however, could hurt them.

She arrived in the first part of the morning. With any luck, Giuliano would be home. She would wait all day to see him if she had to. She knew he would often take a carriage to the center of town where the government met, but doubted he would go this early.

Making sure no one was about, she circled to the rear of the mustard-colored villa using the trees to hide her. They also helped her climb the garden wall. She scaled it and looked in. The garden was empty.

Sitting on the wall, she ate a small lunch of bread and cheese while she waited. She followed her repast with a few sips of water from a goat-skin flask. While she was drinking someone came out into the garden.

Lisa lay down on her stomach and watched. Whoever it was had their back to her and appeared to be holding a rosary, which they fingered as they walked. It looked like Giuliano, but whoever it was wore a black cassock that a priest or cleric might wear. She waited until they had made a circuit of the grounds and disappeared back inside.

Lisa grew impatient. She might wait on the garden wall all day and not see her lover, even if he were there. She decided to take things into her own hands and search the place. It was a bold move, but she was driven beyond all caution by her burning desire to talk to Giuliano.

Letting herself down into the garden, she walked along the wall, crouching behind bushes and trees, to the door she had seen the other figure enter. It was not locked. She opened it and crept in. Now that she was inside, however, she had no idea where to go. She could not cry out. She was on her own. She would have to go by instinct.

Tiptoeing down a long hall with a marble floor and vaulted ceiling, she moved quietly past several richly-furnished rooms filled with Medici family heirlooms. No one was about.

She peered into one of the rooms, which appeared to be a large dining area. There was a long table with a sumptuous tablecloth. The grand fireplace was adorned with bas-reliefs of the Medici crest and stone. Large windows looked out onto the grounds. Full-sized mirrors reflected the light from a grand chandelier. Pictures of Cosimo and Lorenzo and other great men of the family graced the walls. The remains of a meal were scattered about on gold plates. A man in livery was clearing the table. She sneaked past without being seen and continued on her way.

Another open doorway took her past a small study with a beamed ceiling and a dark, hard-wood floor. The walls were decorated with frescos of grotesque motifs such as animals and women, and dancing skeletons. Sofas and chairs sat along the walls, while a desk and chair stood in the center of the room. She could hear servants talking and pans banging at the near-end of the hall. It sounded like it was coming from the kitchen.

She moved in the opposite direction around a corner, and came to a broad, carpeted staircase. Perhaps her lover was upstairs getting dressed. She ascended the steps to the second floor landing.

The rich fabric of the carpet swallowed her footfalls. She made not a sound. Following another hallway, smaller than the first, she passed several bedrooms in different stages of disarray. All were empty.

There was a double doorway at the end of the hall, shining with light from outside. She could hear someone moving around in the interior. Creeping to the glass doors, she peeked inside through the gossamer curtains.

"Giuliano," she said seeing him. Opening the doors, she rushed into the open-air portico.

"Lisa," he stammered in surprise. "What in God's name are you doing here?"

"I had to see you. I had to talk to you."

He ran and closed the doors, after looking down the hall to see if anyone had observed her come in. No one was there.

"Has anyone seen you?" he asked with concern. "You should not have come. No one must find you here with me. It would be very bad for you and your family."

"No one has seen me, but what does it matter? I thought you loved me."

"I do my sweet dove. You are everything to me. What makes you ask that?"

"After what happened in the Loggia. You acted mad."

"I was. I was crazy for you. I wanted you. I wanted you to come away with me. I would have done anything to make you go. We can still go."

"We have gone over this," Lisa replied. "You know I cannot go with you. You promised me that if you could not marry me, you would see that I found a husband. Have you forgotten this?"

"No, but I would rather die before I saw you married to another."

"Then take your knife and slay me here and now. Put me out of my misery."

"Do not talk like that, Lisa. I could easily kill myself, but I could never hurt you. I love you."

"Then keep your promise to me."

"I am sorry, dearest heart, the balm of my torn and pitiful soul. If only we could be together."

He wanted to plunge a knife into his breast and end it all, but he could not take Lisa with him. His hopelessness was deep but not that deep. It would be too cruel to leave her thus, in any case. He was thinking these thoughts when his brother, attracted by the voices, came in.

"What is going on here?" Piero asked, coming in and finding a strange woman on the porch. "Who is this person?"

"A friend," answered Giuliano. "Please leave. We are having a private discussion."

"I could hear you all the way down the hall," Piero replied. "There was nothing private about it. Who is this person?"

"I am Lisa Gherardini," Lisa answered stepping forward with her head held high. "Giuliano and I love each other. We want to get married. Why should you stand in our way?"

Piero's face grew bright red.

"Get that woman out of here!" he screamed. "I will have her and her family flogged for this. Where are the guards?"

"Calm yourself, brother," said Giuliano. "You will do nothing of the sort. Do not listen to this crazy girl. We were only talking about a suitor I have found for her. It is not as you think. So do not be so hasty to embarrass yourself."

Piero was about to respond with more threats, when one of his ministers rushed into the room.

"Your Lordship," the man said with fear plastered on his face. "The French have just invaded."

Chapter 26 – Invasion

Giuliano and his brother had been on the verge of blows when the official came in. Now they were again brothers faced with a common foe, the French.

"Charles has crossed the Alps and is threatening Milan," continued the messenger.

"I knew this would happen," said Giuliano. "Ever since Ferranty died in the beginning of the year, Charles the VIII has been asserting his hereditary claims to Naples. He has been building an army behind the mountains. Now he has unleashed them on Italy."

"Well, it is none of our concern," replied Piero. "It is a long distance away. Let Milan worry about it. The French king was probably lured here by the Sforzas for their own gains."

"Milan will make its own deal with Charles," said Giuliano, "and throw the rest of us to the dogs. What are you going to do?"

"Nothing," answered Piero. "What do you expect me to do? We cannot fight the French."

"Then you must make peace with them."

"We have a treaty. We do not need another one."

"That was before Charles crossed the Alps with an army," reasoned Giuliano. "He will have to go through our territory to get to Naples. Are you going to help him or hinder him?"

"Neither. We are neutral," said Piero.

"I doubt there will be any neutrality in this matter," Giuliano replied. "You will be either with him or against him. If I know the French, there will be little chance of holding the middle ground. You are going to have to decide what to do."

"There will be plenty of time for that," answered his older brother and his father's heir.

When the minister had entered the portico and announced the invasion, things became a bit chaotic. Officials and servants ran to and fro. Messengers and spies were sent out and called in. Secretaries scurried to craft letters and responses. Everyone forgot about Lisa, who had been the center of attention only moments before.

Lisa had left while no one was looking and made her way out the way she came in. Even Giuliano forgot her for the moment. When he turned back to where she had been, she was gone.

She was not sure what it all meant. The Alps and Milan were a long way off. Farther than Lisa had ever been. However, the reaction of the two Medici alarmed her. It was as if she had been privy to all the terrifying details and implications. Invasion was a scary word. The world was no longer safe, not even Florence.

To make matters worse, Piero had found her there and threatened her with terrible things. Would he actually carry them out? Were she and her family in jeopardy? Or would the invasion interfere? Hopefully they had more pressing problems than her.

She was not sure how she and Giuliano had left things. Was he on the verge of killing her and himself? He seemed so distraught. Or had he agreed to help her? She wasn't sure. She was no longer sure of anything.

She hugged her arms about her as though she was cold as she trudged through the busy, narrow streets toward her home. Looking inward at the turmoil that was her mind, she hardly saw the bustling inhabitants of the city going to their daily rounds – selling and buying, drinking and eating, playing and working, the honest and evil, praying and cursing - living their lives as they knew how. Totally oblivious to all around her, she silently made her way home.

Like the previous year, Lisa had stayed behind to close up the villa. Even though darkness was approaching, she loaded the wagon and went the twenty miles to the farm in St. Donato to join the rest of the family.

At the same moment, Giuliano was on his way to the Pallazzo della Signoria. He had to consult with the council and then report back to Piero.

His heart was heavy with worry, but it wasn't the French that troubled him. Giuliano remembered how Lisa had disappeared after the messenger came. He was happy that she was able to slip away and not suffer Piero's anger. He was sure that his brother had believed his story and hoped nothing would come of the affair. He was worried, however, that she had departed without talking with him further. There was still so much he wanted to say to her. Now he would be lucky if he ever saw her again.

To part with so much unsaid, so much undone, was like having a part of him ripped out. Now he tried to cling to it, but it flew off like dust in the wind. He was bereft of a piece of himself, the part that felt joy and peace.

War was at hand. He could see it if no one else could. Piero's complacence would lead to disaster. He had urged his brother to call out the levies and fortify his fortresses with men and supplies. But his brother didn't want to appear hostile to the French. Hearing this Giuliano then counseled that they send envoys to Charles pledging support and a free passage through their domain. This too, Piero, refused to continence, insisting on remaining neutral. Giuliano could do nothing but await the onslaught.

Chapter 27 – Bringing in the Sheaves

While great armies moved across the land to the north and statesmen in Italy's capitols consulted, life in the Tuscan countryside went on as it had for centuries. Farmers harvested their wheat and readied it for market.

September was coming to a close. Lisa had been working in the fields with her stepmother and sisters. She had said nothing to her parents about her visit to the Medici villa.

She cut wheat stalks with a long-bladed scythe and tied them into bundles with twine to dry. When this was done, she sat in the field and thrashed the wheat by hand, separating the grain from the stalk. Finally, the grain was winnowed, using a sieve to shake and toss it until the chaff, or outer casing, was separated from the grain. The chaff was allowed to blow away by the wind. The grain was then put into burlap sacks.

While Lisa took part in all of this activity, her mind was miles away, with Giuliano, her lover, her life. She visited the meadow where they had lain together, but he was not there. She went to the old hay barn where they had spent the night, but there were no poems stuck in the wall. His ghost was everywhere. His flesh seemed forever gone.

It was as if he was dead, but even worse, because she knew he was there, standing, breathing somewhere. Those eyes, those beautiful hands still existed – still touchable, still visible, still kissable - but she could do none of these things, only remember. And as the days turned into weeks, into months, even that memory grew dim.

Oh, if she could only see him one more time. If she could only be with him again for just a moment, then she could die happy. For that was what she wanted to do. Though she went through the motions of living each day, she was actually dying a little bit more each night.

Once the grain was ready, it was taken to St. Donato's monastery, where it was ground into flour at their mill for a fee. The monks ran the mill, which was situated on a nearby stream. Lisa made the trip with her father.

"I have heard grave tidings from the north," he said to her as they drove. It was unusual for her father to talk about current events with her. For some reason, he was making an exception this day. "The French have made their peace with Milan. They will be coming this way soon. I hope it does not lead to war."

"Have such things come to pass?" she asked, concerned.

"Yes, it is very grave, and your young Medici is right in the middle of it with his bungling brother."

"I have not heard a thing from Giuliano," she said truthfully.

"I should hope not," said her father. "They are only trouble."

Lisa said nothing as the wagon bounced down the rutted road to the mill with its burlap bags of grain.

"So you have heard nothing from Giuliano?" Anton asked, skeptical.

"No," she replied.

"Time is passing," he pressed. "We cannot stand idle forever. Bartolommeo's father came by the other day. He said his boy's year of service to the duke will be ending soon. It has been almost a year. He told me Bartolommeo is eager to see you again."

"Oh," she said noncommittally.

"What should I tell him?"

"Nothing, tell him nothing."

"I cannot keep them off for long. I must tell them something. We cannot go on like this much longer, relying on these poor harvests to survive. We hardly brought in a dozen bags. Lisa, we must do something soon."

"I know father. I expect to learn something any day now," she answered.

"We are thinking of staying in the country for a few more months, depending on what happens with the French. Florence may soon not be safe."

"I need to return there to learn what I can. I promise that if I do not get confirmation that Giuliano has procured a husband for me, I will come back and marry the Bonachelli boy."

These words soothed Antonmaria's concerns. The milling went well and they returned to the farm with the year's earnings, which they would supplement with other produce harvested from the farm.

Lisa brooded silently. She began to reconsider things. If the only alternative she had was marrying young Bonachelli or running away with Giuliano, she would surely prefer the latter. But what would happen to her family. More importantly, what would happen to her?

She remembered the youth she had met for a brief time and walked with. He was young, but he was not pleasant to look at - just the opposite. She thought of what it had been like to be embraced and kissed by Giuliano. Then she tried to imagine doing the same thing with Bartolommeo. The thought made her shiver with revulsion. It would be like making love to an animal, a bull or a pig. She could not endure such a thing. Or could she?

If she did not do as they said, her dear old father and her sweet siblings, not to mention Caterina, who had done so much for her when Lisa's own mother died, would more than likely be thrown out onto the street, to beg and scrape the sewers like the most wretched of the destitute. She could not bear the thought of that. She could not live with either alternative. That only left one thing.

But what of Giuliano? Could she do that to him? He loved her. She was sure of that. Killing herself would be the worst thing she could do to him. It would bereft him of hope. He would surely die, either by his own hand or from sorrow. She had to see him again.

Chapter 28 – The Envoys

After passing through Milan, which quickly capitulated to all Charles' demands, the massive French army turned south toward Naples, the target of the French king's lust. Pausing on his way down the Italian boot, Charles sent his royal envoys to parley with Piero. Giuliano was also present.

"King Charles the VIII sends his fondest good wishes," announced the envoy, "and asks the rulers of your great city to support his hereditary claims in Naples won by his great forebears, a just and righteous claim that all truth-seeking peoples approve, including the great city of Milan, your sister and neighbor and friend for many days. The King humbly beseeches the great Piero de Medici to allow the king's army to pass through your territories in Tuscany unmolested. He respectfully asks for a reply to his request in five days, and hopes you will agree with it. Your friendship will be kept uppermost in the King's mind in all future matters here in Italy and abroad."

Piero said nothing at first. He then replied in similar friendly terms that he would carefully consider the matter and send his reply in a few days. He had many men to consult with, all the leading citizens of the city and the surrounding country.

"I will do my best to convince them of their duties," he added.

That being said, the envoys left, after being guests at a lavish dinner party, where they were studiously ignored.

"What am I to do?" wailed Piero later that evening to his younger brother.

"I told you it would come to this," said Giuliano.

"We are neutral. I will explain this to Charles," replied his brother.

"I doubt he will listen," said Giuliano. "If you don't give him the answer he wants, which is total submission, he will attack you. You have done nothing to prepare for such an occurrence, though I urged you to do so."

"We are neutral," insisted Piero. "He will have to go around."

Try as he might, Giuliano was not able to get his brother to ether start building up his fortresses in defense or capitulate. Piero's indecision gave Giuliano a troubling foreboding. He knew things were coming to a head, which made contacting Lisa even more critical. He had to make sure she would be cared for if something happened to him.

A few days later Giuliano made a visit to a notary he knew in the city, one who had done work for his family from time to time.

"Good day, ser Piero," he said in greeting. "How does life find you this fine morning?"

"Ah, very well, grazie," the notary answered. "And you?"

"Molto bene, I cannot complain. How is your son, our friend the great maestro?"

Ser Piero was a tall, but rather frail man in his late sixties and had been a notary in the city for most of that time. He had represented Giuliano's father in several disputes and had a wide network of associates and friends.

"Ah, he is fine," answered the elder da Vinci. "He keeps himself busy, as you know."

"And the great bronze equestrian statue he is working on? Has the work been cast yet?"

"As you know, it is a great engineering feat to make such a large statue, with the horse in motion. My son has had many problems. Fortunately, he has been able to solve them, one by one, as usual. He is now pouring wax into a giant mould to test the technique. It is the talk of the town. Even the French admire it."

"That is wonderful," replied Giuliano. "That statue will be one of the wonders of the world."

"Maybe, some day, who can tell what lies in store for us mortals."

"Ser Piero, I was wondering if you could help me with something."

"Si, Giuliano, anything. Your family and I go back a long way. Any way I can make myself of service would be a great pleasure to me."

"It is a delicate matter."

"I have to be very discreet in my business," said ser Piero. "You can count on this."

"Si, I know. That is why I come to you. I have a friend. She is a very sweet and chaste girl."

"Ah, a girl."

"Si," Giuliano continued. "She comes from a very old and reputable family that has come under hard times. She was promised to a noble young man, but because of circumstances beyond the young couple's control, the young man could not marry her. Her name became besmirched in the process. Now, despite her goodness and virtue, she is without an appropriate suitor. I was wondering if in your capacity as a well-known and highly regarded council, that you might suggest someone. It does not have to be a noble. A commoner of suitable means would also be acceptable, maybe even preferable."

Ser Piero, the notary, had a good idea who the young woman involved was. He had heard about Piero de Medici's ban on the Gherardini family. Rather than making him hesitant to help, it made the elder da Vinci even more eager to comply, for he himself knew the girl.

"Ah, I am sure I can find what you are looking for," he replied. "There are many rich commoners, merchants and travelers, who I am positive, would be eager to meet such a one. I will see what I can do and send word back to you on my progress."

"Grazie, ser Piero, you are most kind. If there is anything I can ever do for you, please let me know."

"There is one thing, sire, keep the French out of Tuscany."

"I will do my best, Signore," answered the third son of Lorenzo the Magnificent.

Chapter 29 – Banishment

Five days from the visit of the French envoys had elapsed and nothing had been done. Piero had met with the Signoria and canvassed the members separately to try and come up with a consensus as to what to do. He wanted either support for calling out more levies to defend the fortresses, or an agreement on complete capitulation. He got neither, chiefly because of the influence of a Dominican priest named Savonarola who had recently come to the city. He told them to pray for Divine intervention. The man was currently just a nuisance. He would soon become a scourge.

Piero, unable to do anything one way or the other with the little support he received from the city's governing body, sent his answer to the king announcing Florence's neutrality.

This did not sit well with Charles, who immediately invaded Tuscany and moved toward Florence and Pisa beyond. Besieging the Fortress of Fivizzano, which blocked his path, he sacked and burned it, massacring all inside.

"What are we going to do?" cried Piero as he met his brother at the entrance to their villa. "The French have invaded! They have besieged my fortress and burned it to the ground! All the defenders, all our brave levies, have been killed! Oh, it is terrible! These are dreadful times."

"You must go to the Signoria," counseled Giuliano. "Tell them that you have to meet with the French King. You must give in to his demands immediately."

"Yes, that is what I will do. I will go myself," said Piero, as if to himself.

"What about the Signoria?" asked his younger sibling. "They will need to be consulted."

"I can do nothing with them as long as that snake Savonarola is in their midst. I will tell them once I have secured peace. Come with me, Giuliano. Help me save our city."

They left for Charles' camp that day. It was late October and the weather had turned cold and wet, with light, constant drizzle and fog. They made their way on horseback with just two retainers and little luggage, guided by one who knew the way. When they were close to the French encampment, they encountered armed sentries who took them to the King's tent.

"Ah, so you have come to speak for yourself," the king said when Piero and Giuliano were led in.

"Si, Your Highness, I have come to explain …"

"I am the one who will do the explaining, my young sir," Charles said, interrupting Piero. "There is no neutrality where my hereditary rights are concerned. One is either with me, a supporter of my cause, or one is an enemy, an obstruction, and will be dealt with as such. That should be very clear to you after what happened to your fortress."

"Si, Your Highness, as you command. I am yours to serve. Whatever I can do for you, I will do."

"You will surrender all your fortresses, including Sarzana, Peitrasanta, Sarzanello and Pisa. Your levies will join my army. You will sign your name for Florence, to a new treaty capitulating and pledging your loyalty."

"Si, Your Lordship, as you command," answered Piero de Medici.

It was a humiliating meeting for both brothers, but it was nothing compared to what happened when they got back to Florence.

When Piero reported the meeting with the French king to the Signoria, Florence's governing body, there was an uproar. All the different factions that could not agree on anything before, now came together to express their outrage at Piero's presumption. Not only had he gone to negotiate without their knowledge or permission, he had given in to every single French demand.

"That is too much! You gave away too much!" some yelled.

"A humiliating national disgrace!" others shouted.

Many complained. "The forts? You gave them all of our forts? We are defenseless!"

"What have you done? What have you done?" more cried.

The chorus of complaints went on for several long minutes, building to a convulsive climax of slurs and hatred. People were hurling things at them and coming toward them menacingly.

"Banish them! Banish them!" the mob yelled in unison.

The Medici brothers left hurriedly under protection of their personal guard and made their way home.

Word of the capitulation and the Signoria's reaction was already known on the streets, which were packed. People were demonstrating their disgust and taking advantage of the situation to cause mischief. Houses were set on fire. Crowds of men ran rampant with knives and swords in their hands.

When the brothers got to the villa they found a huge mob surrounding it. They managed to enter through a side door undetected.

"Quick, we must flee," said Giuliano. "We cannot stay in Florence."

Grabbing only what they could carry, they ran from the building. This included the Medici jewels, millions of dollars worth collected during the twenty-two year rein of Lorenzo, their father.

They left in a nondescript carriage with no crest. As they did, the mob began to loot the villa, taking tables and chairs, paintings and carpets, beds, tableware, clothing, anything that could not be nailed down, and even some things that were.

"Where will we go? I am ruined," sighed Piero, shocked and totally defeated by the reaction of the people he thought of as his children.

"We will go to our villa in Venice," Giuliano answered. "We will be safe there."

He had expected something like this, though he, too, was shocked at the reaction of the citizens. He suspected the evil Dominican priest, Savanarola, of being behind it.

"The kind citizens of our fair city will sow what they reap," he predicted bitterly as they left.

The only worry Giuliano had was for Lisa, but there was nothing he could do at the moment. He hoped that what had been started with ser Piero, would somehow come to pass.

Chapter 30 – The Wedding

Much had changed since Lisa had last seen or heard from Giuliano. Nothing was the same, except for Lisa's loneliness and heartbreak.

The New Year passed bleak and dismal, though it was merrier than the sad, joyless Christmas. Even more depressing, carnival passed without a whisper, dark and silent as a tomb, due to the priest-king, Savanarola's, dictates. The city had returned to God, while the countryside was overrun by the French. Naples had been 'liberated' by Charles the VIII, who was now ruler there.

"You will never guess what has happened," said Lisa's father coming home one evening. "Praise the Lord. The Notary, ser Piero da Vinci, knows a silk merchant in the city who wants to meet Lisa. He is looking for a wife. His last wife died recently having a baby"

"Who is he?" asked Caterina.

"His name is Francesco del Giocondo. He was the silk merchant to the Medici before they had to leave the city. I had lost all hope after hearing that Signore Bonachelli's son had been killed in the war with the French. We have been saved."

"A commoner?" she echoed.

"Yes, but a very rich and prosperous one. He is desirous of not only a spouse but one with an old name. He sounds very eager to meet Lisa."

"How old is he?" Lisa asked from the doorway, where she had been listening to the conversation. "And how many children does he have?"

"He is twenty-nine," answered her father. "Old enough to be a mature and caring husband, but young enough to bear you many happy children. He is not an unattractive man, I hear."

"How many children?" said Lisa again with more force.

"Only one," answered her father. "A boy, I believe."

Putting her palms together, her stepmother looked up at the sky fervently "We have been saved."

"This is Giuliano's doing," said Lisa, recognizing the name da Vinci as a friend of her lover's. "He has kept his promise to me."

Tears sprang to her eyes, not because she was happy to have a suitor, which she had mixed feelings about, but because it showed how much Giuliano loved her. Even though he could not have her for himself, he selflessly gave her another who would take care of her and her family.

Her parents took her tears as tears of sadness at having to marry a man fourteen years her senior. A meeting was soon set up between the parties. Because the whole thing was arranged by Giuliano, her lover, Lisa went along with whatever the suitor, Francesco del Giocondo, wished. He knew nothing of Giuliano's part in the affair.

On their very first meeting she signaled her acceptance of the proposal, as did the suitor. This being settled, a dowry was quickly proffered, the same one Antonmaria had settled on when he thought the Medici youth was a suitor. Lisa's dowry of 170 florins and the San Silvestro farm in the village of Poggio, was not large as those things go, but it was all the wealth the Gherardini family had in the world.

Although the suitor at twenty-nine was quite a bit older than Lisa he was not too bad to look at. He had a distinguished appearance, with a full beard and mustache, and curly black hair. His hairline was receding, but his brown eyes were gentle, with fine, delicate brows. More importantly, he appeared and sounded intelligent and kind. His best feature was his finely-boned hands.

Things accelerated from there. Francesco showered Lisa with gifts, rich gowns and robes, and sparkling jewels, all meant for her to wear and show off before and after the wedding. The wedding dress alone cost more than all the clothes Lisa and her family owned put together.

Her suitor was generous and thoughtful. He dined with the family often over the next few weeks, always bringing gifts for the mother and sisters, and presents for the boys, including a pipe with tobacco for Anton, one of the exotic items from the newly discovered West Indies.

A large gathering of the men from both families took place at the Gherardini residence, where the final terms of the marriage agreement were hammered out in public, before everyone. Things like the dowry amount and payment schedule, and the wedding date were finalized.

A few weeks more and the family would have been evicted for failure to pay the rent, shunned by the community. Now the Gheradinis were the talk of the town, part of a wealthy and well-respected merchant family, their daughter dressed and bejeweled like a queen. The transition was breathtaking. Everything was building to the climatic moment.

The Ring Ceremony took place at the Gheradini home, which had been spruced up and decorated for the occasion. When Francesco took the ring out of its ornate case, there was an audible gasp from the attendees. It was a magnificent five-caret Indian diamond, one of few on the continent. She wore it only for a few minutes. Then it was taken and put into a vault for safe keeping.

The wedding ceremony itself was small and simple, taking place in the basilica in Florence, with a priest and only close family present. It was here before God that they exchanged vows. Even though she spoke hers to Francesco, the man she was marrying, in her mind and heart she was saying them to Giuliano, wherever he might be.

"I vow to cherish you all the days of my life, to love you and serve you and be yours forever, through good and bad. Even though we may be apart, my heart will always be with you. Wherever you may be, I will be yours, always and forever, so help me God, Amen."

There followed lavish and joyous celebrations and festival meals. A lively procession marched through the streets of the neighborhood with music and banners proclaiming the union of the two families.

While this was taking place, the bride with all her gifts and possessions in a wagon, moved from her home to the home of her husband, which at this time was the upper back rooms in the villa of his parents.

Despite all the joy and gaiety around her, and her frozen smile, Lisa's heart was heavy, aching with longing for another. She moved slowly and sedately as if she was an old queen-mother going to her son's funeral, but none of the revelers noticed.

Everything was moving fast, almost too fast for Lisa to comprehend. Although she knew in her mind what was going to happen, when it actually occurred she was ill prepared. One minute she was trying on a ring and riding in a procession, standing before a priest taking her vows, and the next, she was in bed with a man she did not know.

The instincts that stirred her with Giuliano did not move her now. She lay stiff and frigid. It did not matter, however. This was Francesco's third marriage. He knew what to do.

Gently removing her nightgown, he ran his hand over her body. Her nipples were stiff from the cold air. He cupped his hand around her breast and softly kissed her on the mouth. His breath smelt fresh and clean, as if he had just chewed a fruity peel. His hands were washed. His bare arms were well-formed, not muscular but not flabby either.

Lisa did not move through the entire ordeal, though it was not unpleasant. As far as Francesco was concerned, Lisa acted just like the first-time virgin he thought her to be. He treated her like the child she was. But before the act was over and he had done his purpose, he detected something in her, something unexpected, a certain animal urgency, a certain readiness on her part, even something hungry in her love-making that made him realize what a lucky man he was in finding this young woman. If self-satisfaction was a sin, he had just committed a mortal one.

Lisa had felt many sensations in her young life, some pleasant, some not so, but she never felt anything like this. Her mouth popped open when he penetrated her, and a little round 'Oh' came out. She did not know if she liked it or not. It was a rather rude violation of her body, something her lover had never done. It was not exactly painful. For her new husband was as gentle as a groom with a young, shy foaling. But it was not exactly pleasant either.

When it was done, Francesco rolled over and went to sleep. Lisa did not move, but lay there on her back looking up at the ceiling. She woke up on her side, though she did not remember going to sleep. Her mind was numb, her brain a blank. Even though her husband had filled her, she felt empty and used.

Chapter 31 – Mourning

It was 1499. Four years had passed since her wedding night. Lisa had had two children since that time and had grown quite used to Francesco, one could almost say comfortable. Now she was in mourning.

Her third child, a girl, had died earlier in the year and she had still to get over it. So much promise crushed in an instant by a cough. After all this time, it still left her shaking in denial.

The demands of her first two, however, along with Francesco's boy, could not be ignored. So she tightened her skirt, pulled up her sleeves, and went to work, though it did not seem like work to her.

She loved tending her little ones, cleaning them, teaching them, playing with them and nursing them. She loved being the head of her household. She even loved her husband, who was away much of the time in exotic lands buying and selling silk.

Although she had household servants to do the wash and sweep the floors, to cook and dust, she loved doing all of those things herself. Not only that, she did it better than most of the help and had fun doing it.

Lisa always had a little smile on her lips, or in her eyes, depending on where you looked. She seemed to see things - beautiful things, wonderful things - that others could not see. Or was she hearing music from the spheres, a music sublime heard only by the angels in heaven and her.

What she saw was Giuliano - Giuliano kissing her, Giuliano touching her, Giuliano looking into her eyes. What she heard was her lover's voice - whispering to her, singing to her, telling her he loved her.

Everything she had in life she owed to him. He had not only saved her, he had saved her family, who were prospering again. Even if she had not been in love with Giuliano before, just that alone would have made her his forever.

She loved her husband, too, but in a different way. Francesco was wise and kind, and loved her ardently, as was shown by the presents he bought her and the attention he lavished on her. She had even told him about Giuliano and he understood. Together they had brought three little angels into the world. Now one had been taken back to heaven.

It was a cruel cross to bear, but she and Francesco had born it and it had brought them even closer together. Yet it was Giuliano she thought about when she was alone, young, handsome, beautiful Giuliano.

She had heard that he and his older brother had been banished from the city and had fled to Venice. It was a mean fate and it had affected her greatly. She was still mourning that when her baby was taken from her. Now she grieved for each. It was all one big ghastly pain, but she bore it stoically. Some, like Giuliano, would say it made her even more beautiful.

Her husband had cancelled his seasonal trips to the east to be home with his wife during these difficult times. As usual, he lavished rich gifts of clothes and jewels on her. However, none of these things seemed to shake her from her depression. It had been almost a year and Francesco was at his wits end.

"I do not know what I am going to do," he said one day while talking to his notary, ser Piero.

"Is she not well?" asked the lawyer.

"She has not been well since her baby died earlier this year. It was her first girl. She took it hard. She is tired and listless. Nothing seems to make her happy except playing with the little ones. She walks around on the verge of tears in the evening. It is depressing to watch. I do not know what to do."

"How old is your wife now?" asked Ser Piero.

"She just turned twenty this year," answered her husband.

"Ah, almost a woman. You should renew your vows and commemorate it with a painting. Perhaps my son, Leonardo, would be willing to do it. It might be just the thing to cheer her up. He can even include the deceased child if you like."

"I had not thought of that," answered the wealthy silk merchant.

"Oh, it is all the rage," ser Piero informed him. "The nobility, the dukes and counts, have been doing it for ages, but now with wealthy patrons as yourself, anyone with the means can do it. It is especially appropriate if one has married into an old family like you. It is a sign of distinction for the woman to be displayed thus, in a portrait from a famous master."

"I do not know," replied Francesco. "I have not considered such a thing. I will give it some thought and talk to Lisa about it."

"I can talk to my son," said the elder da Vinci. "I am sure he would be delighted to paint your young wife, especially after he has had the opportunity to meet her."

"Do not act prematurely, ser Piero. As I said, let me think it over. I will get back to you shortly."

Francesco left his councilor's office deep in thought. He had seen the portraits of other great ladies in the homes of his patrons and at the City Hall buildings, some of them quite young and beautiful, though none more so than his wife. It certainly would be prestigious to have a painting of Lisa on display on the wall of some grand hall or building.

He had been planning on buying a villa of his own. Perhaps he could hang it there. The more he thought about it the more enamored he became with the idea. He could not have just anyone paint it, however. It must be someone with stature, a famous artist known by all. He knew very little of ser Piero's son, who he knew more as a military engineer than a painter. He would have to ask around for a suitable master. In the meantime, he would talk to Lisa.

Chapter 32 – A Meeting in Venice

Much had happened in the four years since Giuliano had last heard from Lisa. Charles VIII of France had taken Milan from the Sforzas. All this time, Giuliano had been in Venice, living off the family jewels, which were slowly becoming depleted.

He had been in constant contact with friends in Florence, who kept him informed of happenings there. Savonarola, the errant Dominican priest, had been burnt at the stake. Still, the Medici were not welcome.

"Signore, you have a visitor," said Giuliano's man, "Da Vinci, who has just arrived from Milano."

Giuliano had been sitting on a divan looking out his window at the canal. He rose to greet his visitor.

"Buona giornata, Master," said Giuliano. "It is so good of you to visit this poor outcast."

"Ciao, Signore," said da Vinci. "It is good to see you are well."

The visitor was in his late forties, big and broad-chested, with a thick neck and wide shoulders. Tall and clean-shaven, he had light, long curly hair. His chin was square, his nose large, and his eyes sad. He looked muscular, but was dressed like a dandy, with a short, rose-colored tunic, fur collar, and dark-purple hose. A pink cap completed the ensemble

"What can I do for you, Master?" asked the young Medici.

"As you know I have been in Milan as impresario to the Duke Ludovico Sforza. He has had to flee to Germany after the French took the city. I have stayed and made myself useful, but things are in upheaval there and the war is still going on. It was time to leave. The first person I thought of was you, for it was your dear father, the Great Lorenzo the Magnificent, who sent me to Milan in the first place those many years ago."

"Si, I remember. I was but a child," said Giuliano. "I regret I am in no position to employ you. I have no court and no city."

"No, Signore, I do not seek patronage here, though I hope you will soon be restored to your high place in Florence. For I am heading there and hope to find a place to live and work."

"I am sure you will have no problem wherever you go, Maestro. Your name and fame precede you."

"We will see," answered the great painter and engineer.

"By the way," Giuliano said. "What ever happened to the equestrian statue you were creating? Was it ever completed?"

"No, I am sorry to say," replied the painter. "They ended up melting down the bronze for cannons to defend against the French siege."

"That is a pity, Maestro," said Giuliano. "It would have been one of the wonders of the world. Now mankind has been deprived of a great masterpiece."

"Ah, it does not matter," answered da Vinci. "I will create others."

"How is your father these days, ser Piero?" Giuliano inquired, changing the subject.

"He is fine, grazie," answered Leonardo.

"Your father did a great favor for me," the young Medici told him.

"Yes, I heard, the marriage of the Gherardini girl to Francesco Giocondo. Was she a relative of yours?"

"Something like that," answered Giuliano, not wanting to divulge too much.

"I hear she is with child again," said Leonardo, not knowing of the child's death the previous year.

"That is good to hear," said Giuliano. Although he put on a brave face, he was dying inside. These could have been his children. Now he had none. He had no one. He felt totally alone, an outcast, banned from home and family.

"I was wondering, Master," Giuliano continued, "if you could look in on her for me when you are in Florence and extend my warmest regards? Tell her I am doing well and think of her often. Perhaps write me back and tell me how she is doing."

"I should be glad to, Signore."

"Hmm, I wonder if you might do me an even greater favor," said the Medici after further thought. "Could you paint her picture for me? I would pay you handsomely, for I know you do not normally do that sort of thing. You are a great master and not a portrait painter, but she is a special girl. If you saw her, I am sure you would agree. I think you would find her an interesting subject."

"I do not know, Signore. I am very busy with many commissions, but I will think about it. Perhaps I will visit this girl and see for myself. In any case, I will convey your greeting and write of my visit to tell you what I think."

"Grazie mille, Master," said Giuliano. "I and posterity would be forever grateful if you could do such a thing as paint her."

Chapter 33 – The Proposition

That evening, when Francesco returned home from his visit to ser Piero, he kissed his wife as she greeted him at the door. They were still living on the upper floors of his family's home. With their three boys, one from his previous wife, things were getting crowded, although the loss of their daughter would make room for awhile. It was a terrible price to pay, however, for more space.

"What is that delicious smell?" he asked, sniffing the air.

"I have made your favorite, minestrone soup," she answered.

"Ah, I will wash-up and we can have dinner. I have brought some fresh bread. It will go good with the soup."

She did not reply. She did not smile.

"I saw ser Piero, the notary, today," he announced. "He told me about a property that might be for sale. It is in via Della Stufa, near my parents' old home."

She seemed uninterested. Rather than answering, she picked up one of her boys and walked into the kitchen.

"Hurry and wash, the soup will be done soon," she said over her shoulder.

"It sounds like a beautiful place," her husband continued. "It has plenty of room, a large, open dining area, and a beautiful view of the river."

"Hmm," she said in reply.

"How are you feeling today, my dear?" he asked.

"I do not know," she answered listlessly. "I feel nothing. I miss my baby girl."

"We will have others," he replied trying to sound cheerful.

"Not like Piera. She was beautiful."

"Ser Piero mentioned that his son is a painter. He offered to have him paint your portrait. We could hang it in our new home for all of our friends and relations to see. Your cousin, Lucinda Rucellai, has a nice portrait hanging in their villa."

"Yes, I have seen it. She is very pretty."

"Not as pretty as you, Lisa. We should have your picture painted while you are still young."

"And in mourning?"

"You have mourned long enough. It is time for you to go on living. Let us renew our vows and have another child."

"No, it is too soon. I am not ready."

"You are right, my dear," conceded her husband. "First we will buy a new home where we can have many more children and renew our marriage vows. Then we will have your portrait painted by a world-renowned artist, and then we will have another child."

"Do as you wish, husband," Lisa said. "It does not matter to me, but unless you want a portrait of one who cares not for life, who clings to sorrow and death, do not paint me, for I am in mourning still."

"Oh, Lisa, must you be so morose," objected Francesco. "You want to wear your feelings on your sleeve for all to see? Rather show them that you are happy, content with your lot."

"What, happy with the death of my child, content with a grave where a little girl should be?"

"You must get over it, Lisa. It has been almost a year. You have two beautiful children to care for and enjoy, not to mention my son, Bartolomeo, who loves you dearly, like his own mother. You have a home and a husband who loves you, fine clothes and good fare. Be thankful for what you have. Care for those who are still here who need you. Or is it something else you mourn for other than your child? Your young lover, perhaps?"

"I know not what you speak of. It is my child that was lost. None other."

"No, none other than your Giuliano, I'll wager."

"I lost him long ago, when our city turned him out and he had to flee. It is an old story and it is over, as you know. So do not bring it up unless you want to torture me more than I already am."

"No, Lisa, I do not want to hurt you more. I want to make you happy again, your old self before all this misfortune befell you."

"Then be kind, my love. Give me time and space to grieve in my own manner. Perhaps a portrait would be a good idea after all, but not right now."

"Good then," Francesco replied. "In the meantime, I will seek to find a master of renown worthy of such a picture."

Over the next few days and weeks, Francesco canvassed the many art studios in the city, and taverns where artists were known to frequent, seeking the painter of highest repute. Many knew of ser Piero's son and praised his talent, but there were also whispers about the man's habits of homosexuality and his religious heresy. He studied witchcraft, said some. He practices sodomy, said others. A few even said that he desecrated dead bodies by cutting them up and painting pictures of the various parts. Though many said he was a painter of renown, there was much about him that was odd and troubling, which made having him paint Lisa's picture problematic.

Others had mentioned an up and coming artist name Michelangelo, who was currently working on figures for the Piccolomini alter in Florence. He was distinguished for his vibrant colors and the detailed renderings of his subjects. All in all, it seemed that Florence was rich with artists, any one of which could paint his wife's portrait. All he had to do was get her to agree and commission one.

Chapter 34 – An Assignment

Ser Piero made his way to the cloister in the church of Santissima Annunziata, where his son lived with his entourage. He knew that Leonardo had just arrived in Florence and was looking for work. The artist was in his workshop and had just finished with his two students.

"Ciao, Papa," Leonardo said, greeting his father. "What brings you here?"

"Hello, my son, I have news of a possible commission," Ser Piero told him.

"Ah, a military fortification, perhaps, or a battle scene. I would like to do another work like I did in Milan on the convent wall. I would like to perfect the technique."

"No, nothing like that, a portrait of a young lady."

"A portrait! No, never again. Ludovico's sister-in-law, Isabella d'est has been hounding me incessantly since I agreed to do hers. I never should have consented to your entreaties. Now you come again with a portrait? I am no portrait painter. I have no fondness for it."

"But you need the work," insisted his father. "You have not had a commission since you arrived back in Florence."

"I hear Cesare Borgia is in the city," replied Leonardo. "Perhaps he will give me work inspecting his fortresses, or building siege engines for him. Anyway, why would I want to paint this young lady?"

"There are many reasons you may want to paint her picture. First of all, she is pretty, a fresh, young beauty, chaste yet voluptuous. Secondly, her husband is a good friend and client of mine. His wife has lost a child recently. The painting will help restore her well-being. On top of this, these people are not aristocrats or nobility. They are common folk. They will not make ridiculous demands. You can paint her as you wish and not cater to the patron's whims. She has a beguiling smile. If you could capture it, it would be a masterpiece."

"What did you say her name was again?"

"Lisa, Francesco Giocondo's wife. I believe her maiden name is Gherardini."

"Ah, I know of her. Giuliano de Medici mentioned her to me not long ago on my way through Venice. He, too, wanted me to paint her picture."

"Yes, it was Giuliano who helped arrange her marriage to Francesco."

"Si, I remember now. Perhaps I will take a look at this young woman," said Leonardo.

Taking a pen he wrote a short note on a piece of sketch paper.

"Here," he said to one of his young associates. "Take this note to Francesco Giocondo's, the silk merchant's residence, and give it to the woman of the house. I will meet this Lisa."

Later that day a rather flamboyantly dressed young man called on Lisa at her home. Her husband was away. The boy told her he was sent by a friend of Giuliano de Medici's who had a message for her. The message said to meet him at the church of Santissima Annunziata at the sixth hour. He had news from Giuliano.

Lisa arrived breathlessly at the church at the designated hour and looked around frantically for her lover. He was not there, but a large, oddly-dressed man, with long thinning hair approached her with a bow.

"Ciao, Madam. Is your name Lisa Giocondo?"

"Si, Signore. Are you Giuliano's friend?"

"Si, I saw him last in Venice. My name is Leonardo da Vinci. He wanted me to extend his best wishes. He wondered if I would paint your picture for him."

"Giuliano said that? How is he? He is not married now, is he?"

"Giuliano is fine and wishes he could see you. Since that is impossible, he wanted a picture so that your image would be always before him."

"Did he really say that?"

"Yes, but not in so many words. You were all he talked about. He wishes you good tidings and is not yet married that I know of. But you are."

"Yes, thanks to Giuliano."

"He must love you greatly."

"Yes," she said smiling, a tear in her eye. "I guess he does."

Her smile brightened an otherwise dreary day. At that moment, Leonardo knew that he would have to paint her picture.

Chapter 35 – The Outcast

Giuliano walked the long canal, past gondolas and sailing craft bobbing on the quay. The gulls cried forlornly in the darkening sky. He could often be found walking this way at all hours of the day and night. He had to keep moving, like a shark, or he would suffocate in anguish. It was the only thing that gave him peace in his otherwise stormy existence.

His older brother, Piero, spent his days sleeping off the nights of drinking and debauchery. Giuliano did neither and barely slept, afraid to dream. His heart was empty, his soul in turmoil. Despair was too nice a word for what he felt.

His life was on hold, his fate in the hands of others, like his homeland and city. Foreign lords ruled the day. There was a price on his head in Florence. Paid assassins were everywhere, at least in his mind if not in reality.

He thought his longing for Lisa would grow weaker over time, but just the opposite occurred. The longer he was away from her, the stronger his desire for her became, until he could stand it no longer. Yet, there was nothing he could do. To appear in Florence would mean imprisonment or death.

He despaired of seeing her again. The only hope he had in a hopeless sea of days was if the master could render her in oils. He was sure the artist would make it lifelike enough to evoke her presence. Then he could look upon it and live and breathe again knowing that she was still there, her likeness captured in timelessness.

Until then, he wandered the streets and waterways of the half-sunk city, looking for the elusive peace only his Lisa could give him. How often he had cried out her name in agony.

"Oh, my Lisa, where are you now? Are you well? Do you think of me as I think of you? Oh, what am I to do? I am forsaken without you."

Arriving back at their villa after dark, he met his brother, Piero, in the villa's large, open living room. He sat at a long table in front of the huge hearth. It was early and he was not yet besotted with wine. He greeted his younger sibling boisterously.

"Buona sera, brother!" he said. "Have you been out haunting the streets as is your want? Here, join me in some wine. It is a very good year. I have a few friends coming, some very pretty girls. Why do you

118

not stay and enjoy the senoritas. They will take your mind off that Florentine girl."

"Do not speak of her," replied Giuliano. "I am not interested in your puttanas."

"Whatever. Suit yourself," said Piero.

"I am going to Florence. I leave tonight," announced Giuliano, as if making his decision at that moment. "I have to see da Vinci."

"Are you mad?" Piero said. "They would hang you on the spot. Either that or burn you at the stake like they did that heretic priest."

"I do not care," answered Giuliano. "I have to see him. I have to see if he is working on my commission."

"If the Florentines do not get you, the French will," his brother warned. "It is a warzone there. Everyone is fighting everyone else. No place is safe."

"I must see her," insisted Giuliano in anguish.

"Who? Your Lisa? You are mad," Piero said. "I forbid it. I will have you put under guard."

"You have no authority over me here, Brother," Giuliano responded. "I am free to do as I wish. It is I who has been taking care of you, while you drink your life away. Do you know what they say about you? They call you 'the Unfortunate'. What kind of legacy is that after they called father 'the Magnificent'? No, do not get haughty with me or I will have you put out on the street."

Piero said nothing, but snorted a laugh and rose to greet his guests, who had just arrived. Giuliano went upstairs to his room to get ready for his trip.

He planned to leave Venice and travel west to Verona, where he had friends. Then he would go down the spine of Italy to his home city, Florence. Milan was in French hands, his friend Duke Ludovico imprisoned there.

The Spanish and the Austrians were nibbling pieces of his country like scavenger dogs over the corpse of a cow. It was rumored that the Turks would soon attack Venice. It was a good time to go, but nowhere was safe, Florence least of all. He would go there nonetheless.

Anything, even death, would be better than to be separated forever from his love. Even now Lisa's beauty, the feel of her skin, the taste of her lips, was fading from his memory. As the memories faded so did his ability to see beauty in anything. He could no longer taste or feel. His emptiness pervaded everything around him.

Being separated from Lisa made him feel separated from himself. Floating in limbo, he cared about one thing only – Lisa.

Chapter 36 – A Choice

Almost overnight it seemed Lisa had changed her mind. Not only did she like the idea of having her portrait painted, she became happy and gay as she had been before the loss of her child. She could overcome any heartache if she could only see Giuliano again.

When her husband questioned the reason for the change, Lisa credited his words, which she said she had taken to heart. Even if Francesco did not entirely believe the explanation, he wanted to and welcomed the transformation. Now all he had to do was hire a painter.

That night Francesco broached the subject with his wife.

"I have been looking for a master to paint your portrait," he told her.

"I thought Giuliano's friend was going to paint it?" she replied.

"Giuliano's friend?" said her husband, a little taken aback. "Who is that? What has he got to do with this?"

"I thought Giuliano had asked his friend, the Master, to paint it."

"Your old lover, Giuliano, has nothing to do with it. You are confused, my dear."

"I am sorry, my husband. You are right. I am confused," she said realizing her error almost too late.

Her husband continued.

"Although I am loath to offend ser Piero, I am afraid we cannot use his son. I have heard things that make the thought of him painting a young, chaste, religious wife and mother, such as you, quite questionable."

"What, that he is illegitimate and gay? That is no big thing. Almost everyone in Florence has a friend, brother, or cousin that is one or the other. 'L'amore masculino' is so common here that 'Florenzer' is another word for those of that persuasion. Even the pope has an illegitimate child. It is the sign of true manhood in some circles."

"No, it is not that," replied Francesco. "Those things are of no concern to me and are not the true test of a man."

"What then is the problem?" asked Lisa.

"Some say he is a heretic and worships the devil, but there are also more practical matters to consider. Da Vinci is known to be temperamental and unreliable. The Duke of Milan's sister-in-law complains bitterly of his negligence in painting her after accepting the commission. He does not even answer her letters of inquiry. Many of his projects are never completed or delivered. Granted he is a good painter when he puts his mind to it, but he is notoriously unreliable."

"If he wants to paint me, he will paint me," countered his wife.

"That kind of uncertainty might be all right with churchmen and monasteries where things move with the speed of a Gregorian chant, but not for the real world of business and commerce. There, schedules need to be maintained and promises kept.

"There is this young painter, Michelangelo," Francesco continued, "who sounds good. I have seen one of his paintings. It looked very lifelike, with vibrant colors and clean lines. It was very attractive. I could see you painted like that, with your pretty face perfectly rendered in oil. Unfortunately, the artist is engaged sculpting some statue. It is the price one has to pay for hiring such prolific talent. But if he can't do it, I have another in mind."

"I want Master da Vinci," demanded Lisa. "He is the only one capable of doing it. There is no one else of his ability in all of Italy."

"Yes, there is one," said her husband. "A young artist called Raphael, a true master. He is in Urbino, not far from here. He has done many fine paintings and is seeking commissions."

"No, I want da Vinci!" insisted Lisa

"It is I who am paying for it. I will decide who the painter is," said Francesco.

"It is I who must sit for it. I will say who will paint me," answered Lisa.

"Our first argument? Over a painting?" her husband said.

"So be it!" replied his wife standing her ground.

"Be reasonable, my dear," said Francesco. "Our fortunes are rising. Just last year I was elected to the Buonnomini of Florence. It is a great honor to be one of the 'Twelve Good Men' that help govern the city. How would it look if my wife's picture was being painted by an illegitimate, unreliable, homosexual heretic who dissects dead bodies in the middle of the night?"

"I thought you said those things do not matter to you. Do you not care what I want? You want me to be unhappy when my picture is painted? Is that what you want? Because you will have it if you force me to sit for a painting before someone I do not want."

"Raphael is young and enchanting. He would be a delight to sit for. Leonardo is an eccentric old man. He is likely to come here wearing pink tights up to his hips."

"He is a master. He is said to have painted a picture of the Last Supper that is like being in the presence of the Savior and his disciples themselves. He will make me immortal."

"You are talking nonsense, my dear. But if it is immortal you want, you could do no better than Raphael, or Michelangelo, for that matter."

"No, they are mere surface painters. Leonardo will paint me as I am under my skin. He will paint my soul."

Chapter 37 – Languishing

Giuliano was rotting away in Verona. A year had gone by, another was approaching. Unable to go further west due to the French in Milan, and not able to go back to Venice because of the Turks, he was stuck in the city. He could not proceed on to Florence, since Borgia's forces were ransacking the area and selling protection. Nowhere was safe. Instead, he sat in a rundown villa, all that was left of the Medici holdings in the city. He had indeed come to a lowly state.

It drove him mad that Lisa, his love, was a mere three days away down a well-laid Roman road. Yet he could not see her. She might as well have been 10,000 miles away, across the sea in the New World. That was where he wished he was now, that or at the bottom of the sea, for he felt like he was drowning. Being without Lisa was like being without air.

Florence drew him like a magnet. Despite the danger, he felt himself pulled in that direction. Leonardo was there. Lisa was there. Was he painting her picture? Giuliano had to see. It was only his brother, Giovanni, who was also at the villa in Verona, that kept him from rushing down the road toward an uncertain love and certain death.

"It would be mad to ride down there now, with Borgia in Florence," Giovanni counseled him. "He is in league with the French to divide Italy between them."

"Then we should go down and talk to him."

"There is no talking to a man like that," answered Giovanni. "He is ruthless as well as diabolical."

"You exaggerate, Brother," said Giuliano.

"You do not know him. He would use you for his own purposes then turn on you the moment he no longer needed you. Better stay away until he gets his payoff and leaves. Then we can try."

"I cannot stand not knowing what is going on," said Giuliano.

"We can send spies to keep us informed," replied his brother. "The Vatican has many."

"I see you are well versed in the goings-on of the Pope."

"The Papal Armies are our only hope against the French and their puppets, Giuliano. Patience not rashness is called for."

"What would you have me do then?" asked Giuliano.

"Bide your time," answered his brother. "Learn what you can about our enemies in the meantime."

"I need to find da Vinci. He must do the painting for me. I will pay him grandly."

"With what, Brother?" asked Giovanni. "You have spent all of father's jewels. There is nothing left."

"I still have means. There are still some paintings."

"And after that? Will you sell all of father's things to satisfy your mad obsession? There are other women in the world," said the Medici cleric.

"Not like Lisa," answered Giuliano.

"Come to Rome with me, Giuliano. Perhaps you can lead one of the Pope's armies against the French and win our city back."

"It did not go well for Sforza in Milan. There is little glory in a slow death in prison."

"Then come with me to Rome and work with me to get Spain and Venice to join the Vatican in a holy alliance against the French. It will be the best place to be in times like this. You will be closer to Lisa there than you are here. Leonardo may be there."

"Rome you say?" Giuliano reflected out loud. He was intrigued. There were many reasons for going there, not least of all his dislike of Verona and the dirty, rundown villa he was living in. Anything would be better than being cooped up here. Out in the open country, on the road on horseback, would be as close to being free as one in his situation could be.

"Yes, Rome," said Giovanni. "We will go by way of Urbino along the coast. If chance has it that things have altered and an opportunity for going to Florence appears we would be close by. If not, we will simply move on past it to the Eternal City – Rome."

Chapter 38 – A Delay

"What do you mean he is not available?" Francesco shouted at his notary and friend "You promised me he would paint Lisa's picture. You wrote up a contract, which I signed."

"You must understand, Signore Giocondo. My son is a very busy man. He is the chief military engineer for the great Cesare Borgia. He is busy designing and inspecting his lord's castles and fortifications."

"This is outrageous," replied Francesco. "I trusted your word. Your son is said to be untrustworthy, but I put my faith in you, Signore. Now I have been grievously wounded for doing so. You cannot stay in business if your word is no longer good."

"My dear Francesco, we have known each other many years and have worked together amicably all this time. When we wrote up the contract, you knew Leonardo was thus employed by Borgia. It was understood that the work on the painting would be done as time allowed. No other works are being commissioned, but his work for the protection of the realm takes priority, as you can easily understand. What would you have me do? Tell this homicidal illegitimate son of a pope I need his chief military engineer for a portrait of a silk merchant's wife? I mean no offense, my friend, but he would have both our heads. Be patient."

"If it was just me it would not matter, but it is for my wife. She has lost a child. She has grieved hard. We will be moving into a new home. The picture is to celebrate a new beginning. It means so much to us. I know there are many other artists, but she insists it be Leonardo. I do not know why. Maybe someone else has talked to her."

"It is not I, if that is what you are implying. I would never go behind your back like that, Francesco."

"No, I didn't mean to imply… I know you would not do such a thing, ser Piero. But there is another."

He did not mention the name, but thought of Giuliano, Lisa's early lover. Ser Piero knew who he meant but said nothing.

"How long must I wait?" asked Francesco.

"Perhaps he will be free at the end of the year," answered the painter's father.

"The end of the year!" yelled Francesco. "That is terrible. I will get another. I do not care what Lisa says."

"But, Signore, you signed a contract."

Francesco, beside himself, sputtered half obscenities.

"Look," said ser Piero, "I will talk to my son before a fortnight and remind him of his obligation to you. I will also work with Borgia to lighten Leonardo's workload. I will do all these things if you be but patient."

"How?" asked Signore Giocondo. "How will you accomplish this miracle?"

"I know someone Leonardo looks up to and needs support from. He will be very sympathetic to our cause. He has great influence over my son. He will be your advocate."

Francesco returned home later that night bearing a gift for his wife.

"You are late tonight," she said greeting him at the door to their upstairs rooms in his family's villa.

"I wanted to stop and get something for you," answered her husband, handing her a small, velvet-lined, wooden box. "Here, open it."

"Oh, what have you brought me," she said, opening the box rapidly. It was a large, exquisite pearl lying on a green velvet cloth. Taking the black ribbon the pearl was attached to, he tied it around her neck.

"Oh, my darling husband, you should not have done this. It is too much." She admired the neck piece in a mirror. "It is beautiful."

"Not more beautiful than you. It looks lovely on you. I wanted to get you something for what you do for our family, and for going along with the painting."

"I do not deserve it, husband. I will cherish it always and wear it with great pride."

"I talked with the Master's father today. He told me Leonardo is very busy with Borgia's army as their chief military engineer. Have you ever heard of such a thing, a painter building forts? I doubt Raphael or Michelangelo would procrastinate this way."

"Do not fret, husband. He will come when it is time and paint a masterpiece."

"How can you be so sure?" asked Francesco.

"I just know," she replied, thinking of her lover, Giuliano.

Chapter 39 – A Chance Meeting

It was 1502. Following his brother's advice, Giuliano joined him on his journey to Rome. They headed down the old Roman road south from Verona to Bologna, where they spent the night in a monastery, thanks to Giovanni's connections. Sometimes it was good to travel with a man of the church, especially one who worked with the Holy See.

The next morning they were to travel southeast toward Cesena on the coast. They planned to stay there before going south to Urbino, but something happened to change their plans.

When the travelers got to Imoia, the first large town on the way southeast, they learned that Cesare Borgia was there holding court in the fortress. Even more fortuitous, Leonardo was there as well, along with a friend from Florence, Niccolo Machiavelli.

Stabling their horses in an inn where they got a room and changed, Giuliano and his brother went to present themselves to the Borgia court.

Giuliano was courteously received. The Medici crest still stood for wealth and banking, even if their fortunes had taken a downward turn. Many favors were still owed to the reputable old family. In addition, Giuliano's support was critical for Borgia's plans for Florence.

So despite his desire to talk to Leonardo, he wasted several days meeting with and discussing strategies for winning the city back. Not that it mattered. The master was also busy with military matters and painting an aerial map of Florence.

Finally, after almost a week of waiting, word arrived that the master was free and expecting Giuliano to dine with him that evening. The news almost affected the young Medici as if Lisa herself was to dine with him. That is how much the idea of the painting had become an obsession to him. It was no longer just a rendering of her on canvas. It had become the very embodiment of her.

That evening Giuliano and Giovanni went to Leonardo's quarters in a wing of the castle, where he lived with his entourage. The master was already at the table with a young man of about twenty.

"Buona sera, Signore," said Leonardo in greeting. "Welcome to my humble quarters. Thank you for coming. This is my pupil, Giacomo Caprotti."

The youth had curly blond hair and large, vacant eyes, with a fleshy chin and full lips. He hardly looked up as he mumbled a greeting. Giuliano noticed the expensive clothes – the jewels in his hose and a lavish silver cloak with green velvet trim. He wondered how an art student could afford such items. No matter how intriguing the question might have been, however, he got right down to the business of the painting.

"I have wanted to talk to you again, Master, about the Giocondo painting, the girl Lisa."

"Ah, the one with the smile in her eyes," answered da Vinci. "Si, a lovely girl. Nice skin. Good coloring. Si, she would make a good subject, if I get to paint her as I like."

"Paint her like she is," Giuliano urged him. "I must have her image before me, but only if it is lifelike, as if she is there in the flesh."

"I paint none other," said the artist.

"That is the truth," said Giovanni. "I have seen your masterpiece in Milan at the convent of Santa Maria delle Grazie. I must say, it is like being there with the Savior himself."

"Ah, my poor painting," lamented Leonardo. "I do not know how to save it. The oil on dry plaster did not stick well and is chipping off. Someday it will be gone, but then that can be said of all of us. It is what we do and learn while here that counts."

"When will you be in Florence again, Master?" Giuliano asked.

"My service to Casare is very important," Leonardo replied. "It keeps me moving around the country, from Pavia to Urbino, from Milan to Florence. These are difficult times. My skills as a military engineer are much needed. Perhaps next year."

"It means much to me, Master. Your commission will be great."

"The money means nothing to me, only the painting. I will be in Florence in March. Then we will see if there is a painting there or not."

Giuliano said nothing. Machiavelli arrived soon after, and the conversation turned to politics and how to win back Florence. All the Medici youth could think about, however, was Lisa and her portrait.

He imagined it finished with Lisa standing next to it, smiling at him. He pictured holding her and kissing her. He fantasized about taking her clothing off next to the painting and making love to her under the canvas. He was so lost in his daydreams he did not hear the question the new arrival had asked him.

"Where are you going from here, my young friend?" asked Machiavelli again.

"To Rome," he answered, looking at his brother who was holding up his glass of wine. "To The Eternal City!" toasted Giuliano, lifting his glass to the sky and drinking from it.

A short time later, as the men sat and chattered of more trivial things, Cesare Borgia came in person to greet the new arrival.

Handsome and dapper with a full beard and an aquiline nose, Borgia was dressed in black with white trim and a jeweled hat. Eloquent and erudite, he had thin lips and a cruel smile.

"I hope you will stay awhile with me, Niccolo," he said to Machiavelli. "You also, Giuliano. The two of you would not only be great company, but also very useful for my plans."

"I am yours to command," replied the Florentine secretary. "I have been sent by the council for just such purpose, to aid you in your important task."

"And you, Giuliano?" Borgia said looking at the Medici. "Are you so eager to get to Rome that you cannot stay with us for awhile?"

"I would much rather be in Florence, your Excellency," Giuliano told him.

"Perhaps that can be arranged, my friend," replied Borgia. "I wonder if I can have a word with you in private later," he whispered taking him aside.

"Certainly, Signore," said the Medici. "I am at your service."

A few hours later when the guests were getting ready to leave, Cesare Borgia led Giuliano to an upstairs room of the castle.

"Someone is very much taken with you, Signore, and wants to see you. She waits within."

For some reason - perhaps it was wishful thinking - Giuliano thought that Borgia had somehow contrived to bring Lisa there. Without hesitating or questioning, he threw open the door and ran in. There waiting for him was not Lisa, but Cesare's sister, Lucrezia!

Chapter 40 – An Interlude

The door closed behind him. He stood with his mouth open not able to move or speak. Lucrezia wore a golden brocaded gown, with long sleeves and a low neckline that showed more than it should have. Her long golden hair shimmered in the candlelight. She was twenty-two, a year younger than Giuliano, but her sweet face made her look even younger, not more than seventeen. She looked more beautiful than the first time they met.

Giuliano bowed deeply, not taking his eyes off her smooth, white breasts.

"Good evening, Signora," he said without smiling.

"Ciao, Giuliano de Medici," she replied. "I have been thinking of you."

"You have? I have not thought of you since I saw you last. I have no wish to be used for your devious purposes."

"I would not use you deviously, my dear sir," said Lucrezia. "I am serving my brother. I have been remarried as he has arranged. I am now the duchess of Ferrara."

"I am happy for you, my Lady," said Giuliano. "I hope you are happy too."

"I am always happy to see you, my Lord," Lucrezia replied, "But I am not happy with my current husband. Nevertheless, one does what one must. My brother will be very powerful one day."

"And so will you. He has made me see you against my will."

"You came in quickly enough. I did not see you hesitate to enter."

"I thought I was meeting someone else," explained Giuliano.

"And who would that be?" asked Lucrezia

"Lisa, my love."

"Ah, you have a lover. Why are you not with her now? Or is that the one you married off? How gallant of you. You ruin her, desert her, and then you marry her off. How charming."

"How do you know all that?" Giuliano asked. "Do you have spies watching me?"

"You are fun to watch, so earnest and pure-hearted. We are both married now. I can give you much more fun than that other woman." She moved closer to him.

"I love her," said the Medici. Standing straight with his legs apart, he stuck out his chest in defiance.

"I will make you forget her," said Lucrezia, putting her arm around his neck and pulling him into a kiss. Like their first kiss, it lasted for several minutes. As before, after hesitating for a short time, he started to kiss her back.

It had been long since he had kissed a woman, especially one so beautiful. Their faces were pressed so close together that all he could see was a smooth cheekbone and the long lashes of a green eye. Her lips were not as soft as Lisa's, but just as sweet. He could feel her firm breasts pushing against his chest and hoped he would be asked again to kiss them. In the end, he did not have to be asked.

"Yes, you are a very good kisser, Giuliano," she said. "That is what I remember most about you. I am glad to see you have not lost your touch."

He did not answer, but kissed her hard on the mouth again, crushing her to him. Where he was gentle with Lisa, he treated this lusty girl violently. He held her roughly and threw her hard onto the nearby bed. She seemed to like it and pulled him on top of her.

"Yes, my Lord, take me," she moaned. "Do as you wish with me. I am yours."

He pulled her gown down below her breasts. Her rosy nipples stood stiff and ripe. He kissed them and licked them, almost leaving teeth marks. She groaned and grabbed his manhood through his tights. He exploded with a sudden spasm, screaming loudly in ecstasy and surprise. He did not expect something like that to happen so quickly.

She laughed when she felt the wetness of his leotards where she held him firmly. Then she pushed him down and got on top of him. Giuliano had never experienced such handling from a woman, but Lucrezia had studied the art of dalliance and knew about positions that the young Medici had no clue of.

He was in the hands of an artist and she played him like a fiddle. She had several orgasms while lying on top of him. He felt so firm and strong, not like her husband. Giuliano, shocked, got up suddenly in the middle of her last one.

"You are a bad person!" he yelled, his manhood still gorged.

"You are a good lover," she replied with mirth. "It is a shame you waste your youth waiting for someone you cannot have."

"I will have her. It is my one desire."

"Then go to her and make love to her like you did to me and she will be yours."

"You are a strange one. You make love to me then tell me to go make love to another?"

"I would love to be there with you so I could make love to both of you."

"You are bad," he said again.

"And what are you, a saint? You are so self-righteous, Giuliano de Medici. You think you are better than I? You lust after a married woman and have just made love to another. You are just as much a sinner as I am."

"You are evil. I should not have lain with you so. I am sorry. It will not happen again."

She laughed loudly.

"Do not tell me," she replied. "Tell your little sweetheart."

"I feel sorry for you that you will never know love."

"Who needs love when one can have so much fun without it. I will never forget you, Giuliano."

He hurriedly left the castle hoping none would see him. He castigated himself all the way home. He tried to drive the whole thing out of his mind with drink, but that only made the memories more insistent and vivid.

Chapter 41 – The Assassin

Giuliano made his way to the inn where he was staying, weaving his way through the empty streets alone. He had a sense someone was following him, but whenever he turned to look, there was no one there. Still, he could not shake the feeling of being pursued.

He dismissed the idea and continued on his way. After all, he could think of no reason a person would want to follow him. He was not known in these parts and no one from Florence knew he was there. He had announced his plans to no one. He had enemies, but none here that he knew of.

It made no sense. He had not been anywhere since his arrival except the castle and the pub, nor had he shown his purse in public. Perhaps it was a thief waiting for a quiet spot to rob him. He grabbed the hilt of his dagger. Perhaps he should oblige the scoundrel, if that is what it was.

He picked up his pace. Going out of his way to lose anyone that might be following, he ducked down a side street and ran up an alley. Then he back-tracked and ran around the corner of a building. There he stopped and listened.

Peering around the edge of the building, he saw someone approaching. It was a large man in a gray cloak walking cautiously up the alley. When he saw Giuliano, he looked startled and started to run toward him. The young Medici turned and fled down the street in the opposite direction as fast as he could go. The man had a sword.

The Medici did not look back. Jumping over barrels and boxes like a gazelle, he did not stop until he had gone several blocks. He was out of breath and totally disoriented. Reaching the edge of the city, he hid in an old barn full of hay.

Getting his breathing under control, he looked out a crack in the wall and checked the road. The moon was full. There was no one about.

He stayed hidden for what felt like several hours but could only have been one. Then he crawled out of his hiding place, got his bearings, and made his way warily to the inn. He had decided to leave Imoia that evening. His brother could follow the next day.

It was after midnight when he arrived at the inn. Surveying the building cautiously and making sure no one was there waiting for him, he crept into the stable and saddled his horse.

Just as he was about to mount, someone burst into the barn. It was the assailant. He was big-boned and bearded, with a barrel-chest and broad shoulders. His long arms seemed to reach to the floor. He pulled his sword from its scabbard and bellowed like a bull.

"Die Medici!"

Running at Giuliano, the man thrust the tip of his sword at the Medici's mid-section. Giuliano sucked in his stomach and twisted away, knocking a bale of hay in the attacker's path. When the man reached down to push it away, Giuliano grabbed a heavy bridle from a peg on the post next to him and swatted his assailant in the face. The blow knocked the man back and off his feet.

While the man was down, Giuliano, jumped on his horse, kicked its sides, and rode out of the barn at top speed. As he passed the attacker, who had gotten to his feet, horse and rider knocked the man back into a mound of hay, where unfortunately, there was a pitchfork.

Giuliano rode out of town with only the clothes he had on his back. He and his brother had planned to go on to Urbino, so that's where he headed. Every so often, as he galloped down the highway, he looked behind him expecting to find a rider chasing him. Each time he looked, however, the road was empty.

He arrived at his destination several hours later at dawn, with no further incident. Spending the rest of the morning in the cathedral, he fell asleep in a pew.

"Is this how you thank the Lord for his gifts?" a voice said.

Giuliano started up and stared at his brother. Giovanni smiled back, laughing.

"You look like you have had a rough night," he observed. "Why did you leave Imoia so suddenly last night? I thought we were to go to Urbino together. You disappeared as if the devil was after you."

"I was attacked," answered his younger brother. "Someone was following me, a big man with a sword. I ran from him and thought I got away but when I came back to the inn to get my horse, he attacked me. He tried to stick me!"

Giuliano was indignant at the thought that someone would do such a thing. He could think of nothing that could have provoked such an attack. He wondered if Lucrezia or her brother were behind it.

"Unless…It is unthinkable!" he exclaimed in a huff. "I had the most horrid experience after you left. Borgia told me someone wanted to see me. I thought it might be Lisa, but it was his sister, Lucrezia."

"Ha ha, how could that be so bad?" laughed Giovanni. "I hear she is very comely."

"She is horrible. I scorned her advances. I wonder if that is her way of getting even."

"I doubt that very much, Giuliano," said his brother. "She is much too smart for that. Anyway, she would do nothing behind her brother's back like that."

"Then who? I did not go anywhere, except to the castle with you and a tavern for a few drinks. Then I went directly home. No one else knows that I am here. No one here knows me. Why would someone come after me like that, unless it was Borgia's doing? He is a dangerous man, as you said."

"That is true, but why would he want to harm you when he needs your support? Perhaps you simply offended someone in the drinking house and do not remember," suggested Giovanni. "Or maybe it was a thief wanting to pick your pocket. You were in the wrong place at the wrong time."

"No, this person knew my name and yelled it out. 'Die Medici,' he said."

"It sounds like someone was trying to assassinate you. Most probably it is someone from our home town."

"Someone from Florence?

Giuliano thought for a moment. Then someone came to mind.

"Ah, perhaps you are right, but not for the reasons you think. This was not political. It was not a military or courtly person who attacked me, but one you would find on the street, perhaps the docks. He had a seaman's sword. This was personal."

"Maybe it is one of your enemies from Florence," replied Giovanni. "It has come to this. They hunt us even when we are not there."

"Perhaps someone knew I was coming and decided to preempt my arrival."

"That may be," said Giovanni. "But Brother, I have sad tidings I must tell you about."

He paused for a moment and collected himself.

"Our older brother, Piero, is dead. He drowned in the Gariglioano River fleeing the aftermath of a battle against the Spanish."

"That is a pity," replied Giuliano, stunned but not overly surprised. "His drinking and whoring would have soon killed him anyway. Perhaps it is best this way, although it would have done more for his name if he had died running to battle rather than away from it."

"Ah, but that is the way it was with our unfortunate sibling," Giovanni said. "Quickly then, we must go to Rome. Only there will we be safe."

Chapter 42 – The Arrival

"Come, come, hurry, Lisa" said Francesco to his daughter. It was early March, 1503. The head of the year had come and gone with little fanfare. The Feast of the Annunciation of Mary was about to begin. "The Master will be here soon. You must look your best. Wear your wedding ring and your pearl necklace. You must be the epitome of culture for your painting."

"You should let the Master decide…"

"Hurry, Lisa," cried her father cutting her off. "Do you want to be half dressed when the Master gets here? Louisa, help her."

The servant did her best to help her mistress dress, but it still took forever. She had just finished when da Vinci swept into the room.

His hair was starting to recede from his temples. He was still clean shaven, with a square chin and a thick neck, but his eyes were sadder and watery. His broad chest and shoulders were getting less broad, with more fat than muscle. Dressed like a dandy, he wore a short taffeta gown with velvet lining, and a dark-purple cape. The cape had a wide collar and velvet hood. Dark-purple stockings completed his wardrobe.

Lisa curtseyed and Francesco bowed.

"No, no, no!" yelled da Vinci, looking at Lisa. "That will never do!"

Lisa, knowing that what she had on was not what the painter wanted, ran into her room to find something less ostentatious and more everyday. The painter followed, upsetting the servant who had gone to help her. Francesco, already intimidated by the great man's presence, stood mute and helpless.

"Show me what you have," demanded Leonardo. "Throw it on your bed here."

Lisa went through her closet and chests, throwing everything she had on the bed, tables, and chairs.

"Here, that brown cloak with the rose highlight, show it in front of you," Leonardo demanded. "Yes, hold it out. Ah, it is exquisite, with all its folds, the way the garment flows and billows. The light catches the vertical weaves and pleats just right. The mustard-copper sleeves ripple and shine with a striking silky luster. Yes, this will do splendidly. We will wear that.

"And the dress with the pleated bodice and gold embroidery. It is very dark and will go nicely with the cloak. The low neckline will be just revealing enough. And the scarf, we will have it covering your left shoulder.

"Please, my dear. Take off your jewelry," da Vinci requested. "We will paint you with none, nothing to detract from your simple beauty. We will put a gossamer veil over your long straight hair as a mark of your virtue. I will paint it so transparent it will be almost impossible to see."

Like Mozart with several of his compositions, Leonardo could see the whole piece completed in his mind before he even started to put it down on canvas.

"That is enough for now," said the Master. "We have what we need to start the work. I will paint you on the veranda. We will start tomorrow mid-morning."

With that he swept out of the house as quickly as he had come in.

Everyone was breathless with questions. Lisa told them everything – how he had picked her clothes, how he had told her to sit and pose, when they would start.

Francesco was having second thoughts. He was annoyed that he was to have no say in the painting, and that the master wanted to paint his wife like a servant girl, not the head of a wealthy merchant's household. He wondered if someone else was dictating how it was to be, not the painter but someone pulling his strings. And when he thought about who that might be, he turned white with anger.

'Giuliano's friend,' she had said when he first mentioned the painting. He was starting to suspect what that might mean. It did not take much thought to figure out who was pulling the painter's strings, his friend the Medici.

Francesco had not heard from his man, which meant that his task had not been completed. Otherwise, he would be here demanding his payment. The man was either dead or still at work. He hoped the latter but he had to know for sure.

Later that night after Lisa had gone to bed, Francesco put on a large overcoat and a slouch hat that covered much of his face. It wasn't a perfect disguise but it would make it difficult for his friends and acquaintances to recognize him.

Making his way to the rougher part of town near the docks along the riverside, outside the city walls, he entered one of the more notorious of the local taverns, frequented by sailors and dock workers. The place smelled of urine and spilt beer. He found a space at an empty table in the corner and observed the room.

The chances of his man being there that evening were slim, especially since their business called the fellow out of town. He could have returned by now, however, and the odds were better than 50/50 that if he had, he would be here. So he ordered a pitcher of ale and waited. His patience was paid off sooner than expected.

A brawl erupted when one man punched another man at the bar. The man, who had been punched, jumped off his stool and hit his attacker on the top of the head with his fist formed like a hammer. He kept hitting the man so rapidly it was as if he was pounding him into the ground. The other man could not reply. He tried to run but he was driven to the floor unconscious. The winner of the short battle was the man he was looking for.

While they dragged the unconscious man out of the bar, Francesco raised his glass to the victor, who looked up and spotted him. He came over to Francesco's table immediately.

"Won't you join me, my friend," Francesco said as the man approached.

"Do you have my money?" the fellow asked as he sat down.

"Did you finish the job?" the silk merchant inquired, pouring the man a glass of ale.

"He got away," answered the man.

"What do you mean, he got away?"

"He was traveling with his brother, the priest. They were staying at an inn in Imoia. I followed them to the Borgia's castle and waited until they left and separated. Then I followed the subject as he made his way home alone. He was wary for some reason. He started to run. Even though he could not have seen me, he ran like a scared rabbit. He is a slippery one. I lost him. He must have run clear out of town. So I waited at his inn for him to return, which he did later that night.

"I had him trapped in the stable and went at him with my sword, but he was a tricky little piece of scum and came at me with a pitch fork."

He showed the wounds from the tines in his backside to reinforce the lie and hide his shame.

"He will not get away so easily next time," he vowed.

"Then I will pay you next time," said Francesco. Standing up, he threw a few coins on the table and walked rapidly out of the tavern. The man did not follow him, but scooped up the coins and finished the bottle left on the table. He would try again.

Chapter 43 – The Sitting

The morning rose overcast and humid, with a soft breeze to counter the heat. Da Vinci arrived as promised, telling the mistress of the house he would not paint her that day. He was here to set up.

He had decided to paint Lisa in the covered loggia at the south side of the villa, with the hills and river in the background.. His companion, Salai, brought in a thin-grained plank that had been cut from the center of a poplar tree, larger than usual for a household portrait. He would paint the portrait on this panel of wood

Leonardo immediately applied a thick primer coat of lead white.

"Why do you not use your usual mixture of gesso and chalk?" asked his assistant. Known as Giacomo Caprotti, Gian, for short, Leonardo called him Salai, for little devil.

"I have none of the gesso, since you neglected to obtain it for me as asked," answered the artist.

"What will you use for the undercoat?" asked Salai.

"You are full of questions today, Salai," replied Leonardo. "But if you must know, I plan to use white pigment. It will reflect back the light that makes it through the many fine layers of oil better. It will create an excellent translucent glaze. I will apply it over time to enhance the painting and give the impression of depth and luminosity, to add volume. I call it fumato. This painting will be a quintessential example of the technique."

Salai nodded as if he knew what the painter was talking about. More Leonardo's lover than a student, he could dash out poor imitations of the master's paintings when he needed a few lire.

Lisa watched from the sideline. Once the primer had dried, the artist began to work on the background, painting the landscape of rocks, fields, and water, with fine delicate brushstrokes. He seemed to be enmeshed in his own little world, making no sound, gazing off into the distance, seeing all that was there and painting even more.

The following day Leonardo posed Lisa. He sat her fully dressed, in a straight-back, heavy chair. Then he studied her for some minutes with his chin in his hand from different angles, placing her so that the light from a rear window fell on her at an angle. Then he stood back and observed some more. Finally, he shook his head and held Lisa's shoulders.

"Here," he said, turning her body in the direction he wanted. "Twist your torso like this, per favore." He then rotated her head toward him. "It is as if you are turning to greet your lover, who has just come into the room."

She smiled.

Then he started to paint, never a line, only contours and vague forms. A faint figure was beginning to emerge. After a while, he stopped and pondered his subject some more. He started to paint again. Then he stopped and put the brush down.

"Something is not right," he observed. "Your hands, let us rest them on the arm of the chair. Si, like that, buono."

"Smile," he added, grinning at her. This smile was not as genuine as the first for some reason, but the artist said nothing.

Each day that he came, a little more of Lisa's face was revealed. He painted with soft, deft strokes, never delineating an image with a sharp straight line. Sometimes he smudged an edge or color with his thumb or finger tips, to soften the contours even more.

Lisa was mildly surprised that he only painted her on gray overcast days or in the early evening as the light was fading. He told her it made her face softer and more delicate. Another thing that intrigued her was that he only worked when the light came in from the high left of the veranda.

He painted the contours of her cheeks and lips with soft transitions of tone that veiled the many layers of paint and varied as the angle of light changed. The picture seemed to come alive as it grew. The use of shadow on Lisa's face, done with a brown glaze over a pink base graded smoothly, looked even more lifelike.

"How do you do that, Master?" Gian asked after studying the portrait. "How do you get such realistic colors and textures?"

"From years of study and practice," replied da Vinci. "If you worked on these things as hard as you do making trouble and causing mischief, you would be able to do it yourself. But I will tell you. Who knows, you might learn something.

"First, I use a small proportion of pigment mixed into the oil to make the glaze, like this, see? For shadows on the face, I use an iron and manganese mix, creating a pigment that is burnt-umber in color and absorbs oil well. It is my own technique, which I have pioneered."

"Yes, I know, Maestro. That is why you are so renowned. I will remember this and practice as you say."

"Good, Salai, now please get me a glass of wine."

Leonardo's brushstrokes were so delicate that they were virtually imperceptible. Over time they would be up to thirty layers thick, but that would be after years of working on it. It was to be a portrait of the human emotions. What was missing was any emotion at all. Where was that expression that had first captivated the artist, with the mysterious hint of a smile?

Lisa seemed far away as she sat for the painting. Her eyes were vacant. Her mouth was set firm in resignation. She had never felt so far away from Giuliano. Her heart went out to him, leaving the rest of her empty.

In an effort to cheer her up Leonardo employed people to play and sing for her. She smiled politely and appeared to enjoy the music, but the eyes remained blank. Jesters were brought in to make her merry but they only made her giggle a few times. Her mouth laughed but her eyes did not. It was as though he was painting a picture of a picture, not a real, living person.

Then, in early October, just as suddenly as the work began, after it was starting to really take shape, everything stopped. One day Leonardo just failed to arrive. When he did not come after the second day, Francesco sent a messenger to ask why. The Master answered that he had been interrupted by a very important commission, which he could not ignore. Apparently the new commission, which according to the contract should not have occurred, took precedent. The artist could not say when he would be able to continue the portrait.

Francesco was dumbfounded and objected strenuously to both Leonardo and his father, but to no avail. The new commission was for a battle scene for the Florence council hall, in the Palazzo della Signoria. The new painting would be called the 'Battle of Anghiari', and would be painted on the 147-foot west wall. It was a magnificent setting in a room seating the 500 members of the grand council and would be viewed by all.

It was a substantial commission, much more than Lisa's portrait, and more prestigious, thus the change of priorities. Full of blood and gore, it would be a far cry from the warm and peaceful picture of a young mother looking placidly at the viewer.

Hearing this, Lisa became sullen and refused to talk to anyone, much like when she was first told she could not see Giuliano. Although sitting for it had made her sad, the painting was all she had that tied her lover to her. Now she did not even have that.

Not only had the painting not helped, it had made things worse. She was lost in a sea of sorrow again and her husband could do nothing to save her from drowning.

Francesco, realizing what was wrong, was having second thoughts about attempting to harm Giuliano. He finally understood that Lisa's old lover was the real reason for her sadness and that only Giuliano could help her.

He tried to contact his henchman to pay him off and tell him not to pursue the matter. He returned to the tavern several times but could not locate the man. He hoped that he could find him before he acted, or that the assassin would give up on the assignment on his own. He had little hope of either occurring.

Francesco kept working on da Vinci to get him to continue work on the painting. He also attempted to get Giuliano back to Florence, not to have him assassinated, but to help persuade Leonardo to return to the portrait. He realized that Lisa's happiness and well-being depended on accomplishing both goals.

Chapter 44 – A Job Unfinished

Because of the weather and the bad traveling conditions, Giuliano and his brother remained in Urbino, where they obtained lodging at the church. After what had happened in Imoia, Giuliano started wearing a sword. It was given to him by his father. He had kept it in a case with his wardrobe.

He had used it often growing up, practicing with his brothers and their family sword master. He was better than average due to his quick reflexes and excellent hand-eye coordination. He made a good student and had mastered not only the fine art of sword play, but even more importantly, the principles of footwork and balance. He certainly hadn't imagined ever having to use it short of battle. Now here he was walking down the street with it hanging from his side.

He wasn't alone, although the streets were deserted and he had no companion. It was a dark night with a hard rain, which Giuliano rather enjoyed. The hot, damp, darkness matched his mood, which was anything but peaceful. He was actually hoping the assailant of the previous night would come back so he could teach him a lesson. He hadn't counted on two attackers.

Orlando, the man Francisco had hired, remembering what had happened to him the last time he tangled with his target, had enlisted an assistant. Jacque was an out of work Swiss mercenary, who had been dismissed for fighting and insubordination. He was even harder-up than his mate, and would have done anything for the price of a meal. He was making more than that this night.

Giuliano didn't see them lurking behind the corners of two buildings on the street he was walking down, one on his right, one on his left. They came out of the dark with a yell. The noise actually alerted him in time to pull his sword from the scabbard.

"Die, Medici," said Orlando, a dark, heavy-set man wearing a thick, grey cloak and slouch hat. The only thing Giuliano noticed, however, was the curved cutlass in his right hand.

The other man, taller and thinner, was dressed in the tattered and torn remnants of a Swiss uniform. His face was covered with black stubble and sores. He was armed with a heavy truncheon that he raised over his head.

Giuliano parried Orlando's clumsy thrust with his rapier, and countered with two swiping strokes of his own, right, left. One caught his assailant on the cheek, immediately making a gash that started bleeding profusely. It oozed down the side of Orlando's face. He stopped momentarily and grabbed his cheek.

At the same time, the other man swung his bat at Giuliano's head. He ducked away at the last moment and jabbed his sword forward several times, just missing the man, who backed away.

Orlando, who was stunned but not incapacitated, yelled in anger and attacked. Slashing his broadsword from right to left, he ran at the Medici. Giuliano moved back out of reach, but kept his sword on guard over his head and pointing forward. It was a move his father had taught him. It was not only a good defensive position, it confused most opponents that were not familiar with the stance.

The sight of his own blood had enraged Orlando. His anger made him careless. He threw caution to the wind and barreled at the Medici hard, forcing him back. Instead of continuing to back-up, however, on Orlando's next lunge, Giuliano ducked beneath it and thrust his sword forward. His opponent, not expecting the move, ran right into the point of the Medici's blade, impaling himself through the stomach.

Giuliano pulled his rapier out of the dying man just in time to block another downward strike of the bat. The sword snapped in two on impact with the thick wood.

Without thinking, the Medici grabbed the end of the bat and brought the hilt of his broken sword down on his attacker's head. The strike drove the metal into the man's skull, breaking bone and skin. He went down hard and was unconscious before he hit the ground. Throwing his broken sword in the dirt, Giuliano made his way back to his room.

All the way to the church, he looked behind him furtively for anyone who may be following, though he doubted either of his assailants would be getting up any time soon, if ever.

He felt good, strong and resolute, almost invincible. Once the nervous energy wore off, however, and he realized how close he had come to being killed, he sobered up and actually started shaking. It was more from exertion than fear, but it was disconcerting nonetheless.

It had all happened so fast he hadn't had time to think. It was all over in a blink of an eye, but it would remain in his memory for the rest of his short life.

He calmed himself and wondered again, who could have hired them. They were clearly strangers and a second robbery was too much of a coincidence. They had to be assassins for hire. But for who?

Lucrezia? Would she actually stoop to such a thing, over a little tiff? He tried to remember how they had left each other. They'd had sex. Would she try to kill him for that? Was she afraid he would tell someone?

It was her brother that brought him to her. Was Cesare up to something? He seemed friendly enough last time they met. He had wanted Giuliano's support. There was no friction there, unless he totally misread things. He trusted his ability to read people. In any case, it would be foolish to blame either of them unless he had irrefutable proof.

Who else would have it in for him, Francesco, Lisa's husband? No, the notion was preposterous! It made no sense. A silk merchant hire assassins to kill a Medici? Not in the most wild romance novel now the vogue would you find a plot so inane. Then again, they were rivals for Lisa's love. Perhaps her husband knew about their rendezvous. Maybe he had spies about to watch her. How much could he know? Did Lisa tell Francesco that she still loved him?

These questions and others plagued Giuliano's mind as he made his way back to the lodging he and his brother shared. Perhaps it did not matter. He had taken good care of the assassins. They would not be coming back. Still, he had to stay on guard. He needed another sword.

Chapter 45 – The Battle

Leonardo was focused on his new project, to the total exclusion of all else, including the portrait of Lisa. It had completely left his mind. He was totally engrossed in the battle scene he was to paint.

The painting itself had become a battle, a battle against the elements, against time, against his own need for perfection. What had started out as a glorious idea had become a struggle and he had hardly started to work on it.

It began well enough. He had designed and constructed the platform that he would need to work on the wall. It was a scissor-like contraption that moved back and forth, as well as up and down, so he could stand and reach every inch of the 147-foot surface.

He next bought eighty-eight pounds of flour to make the paste he would need to stick up his preparatory drawing, a cartoon of the battle scene. He was looking forward to the drawings in which he planned to show a wide range of human emotions – anger, grief, pain, hatred, terror, pity, and the throes of death.

He had seen plenty of death in the morgues and hospitals he haunted at night, looking for cadavers for dissection. He knew every muscle and nerve in the face and how they distorted the lips and widened the eyes, opened and closed the mouth, and thrust forward the chin. He would use all his knowledge of anatomy to draw the bodies in action, being stabbed and trampled, impaled and decapitated. He used several of his own horses for models in the cartoon.

Work was slow and tedious. Leonardo was haunted by what had happened to the Last Supper painting, how the dry wall on which it was painted flaked. The same thing was sure to occur here in the council hall.

When he was ready for the painting itself, after many had seen and commented on the exquisite composition of the cartoon - some even making copies of it - he made the whitewash for the base and started to paint. But just as with the painting of the Last Supper on the wall in the convent in Milan, the problem with the oils not sticking on dry plaster reoccurred.

Leonard was beside himself. He tried Greek pitch and distilled turpentine. When that failed to have the desired effect, he tried resin and wax with linseed oil. It was all to no avail. The paint could not be prevented from flaking off the dry wall.

At one point, he lit fires beneath the mural to try and dry the paint more quickly. It had little effect. The more he worked, the more frustrated he became. He was also having trouble with the paymaster, who insisted on paying him with small coins.

"I am not a penny painter!" he objected strenuously.

The painting was far behind schedule. He was on the verge of quitting many times. However, when he raised money and attempted to pay back his fee and abandon the project, the chief magistrate of the city refused the money and talked him into going back to work. A new contract was written, stipulating a finish date of February 1505. The way things were going, however, there was little chance of meeting that deadline either.

To add to the artist's consternation, the council had just hired his chief rival, the young Michelangelo, to paint another scene on the opposite wall of the council hall. Not only were their styles diametrically opposed, the young hunchback had shown utter disdain for the older master, treating him with undisguised contempt when they first met.

Leonardo could not stand the man and thought he was a slovenly, uncouth upstart. Now he had to work day and night with him standing not a hundred feet away. It was supposed to be another battle scene, but Michelangelo was painting dozens of nude men bathing in the Arno River. Leonardo was offended.

"That unwashed, disheveled, petulant idiot," he fumed. "All he can paint is nude men and straight lines."

Salai, who actually liked Michelangelo's painting, said nothing.

Behind schedule, harassed by paymasters and council members, tired of trying to keep the paint from chipping from the wall, and daily insulted by his rival, Leonardo was ready to walk away from the project. The last straw came when a violent rainstorm blew open the doors of the council chamber and all but ruined his painting. He cursed the day he had taken the commission. Leonardo needed a lawyer.

Chapter 46 – A Painting Unfinished

Ser Piero, Leonardo's father, came from a long line of notaries. All his sons but Leonardo were notaries. The fact that he was illegitimate may have had something to do with it, but Leonardo had never showed much interest in the occupation. In any case, he had a precocious talent for drawing and went to a master's studio as an apprentice at a young age instead.

Frustrated with the battle scene, Leonardo visited his seventy-eight-year-old father at his new home on the Via Ghibellina, where he lived with his twelve children and fourth wife.

"Father, I am being tortured with this city council commission," he complained.

"It is a lot of money," answered his father. "It would be worthwhile to complete it as soon as possible. You must be almost finished by now."

"No, I have had one setback after another," replied Leonardo. "It has been chipping off like the Supper. Now it has been ruined by the recent rains. The place leaks like a sieve. Not only that, but that lout, Michelangelo, is working on the opposite wall. I have to stare at his stupid nudes all day."

"I thought you would like that," said his father, who did not approve of 'l'amore masculino'.

"No, it disgusts me," replied Leonardo. "It is offensive to discreet tastes and not for public display. The man is a buffoon."

"I hear he is very religious, a celebrant."

"That just goes to show how sick and depraved he is."

"Did you come here to complain about Michelangelo?" asked ser Piero.

"I want out of this battle project," his son responded. "I am done with it."

"You have a contract. If you leave with it unfinished you will have to pay back all the fees and forfeit the work."

"Whatever. I can make the money back. They can have the damned thing."

"What will you do? You will have problems getting another commission if you leave this one unfinished. The council is sure to complain and blackball you. No one will want to hire you after that."

"We will see," said Leonardo, angrily.

"I think it will be best if you disappear for a short time. Why do you not take a holiday from Florence. You need the rest. I will tell them the French have summoned you. It won't be long. Why do you not go to Piombino. There is someone there who would love to talk to you. Perhaps he will have work for you."

"Piombino, what is there?"

"Not what, but who," replied his father. "Your great patron, Cesare Borgia, is there for one."

"I am not sure I want to see him again, after what he did in Senigallia."

"What is that? I have not heard."

"Few have. It is kept quiet out of fear. The madman killed the council members and pillaged the town for not complying with his wishes quickly enough. My good friend Vitellozzo, who had lent me the book on Archimedes, was one of the victims. It was terrible. No, after witnessing Borgia's horrors I would as soon not see him again."

"If not Borgia, perhaps another would be much more to your liking, your friend the young Medici, for instance."

"Ah, Giuliano, but what could he do for me?"

"He has work for you, if I am not mistaken."

"I wonder of what nature."

"You will have to ask him. He is still banned from Florence. You will have to go to him if you wish to find out what it is."

"The Medici would make a good patron," Leonardo confirmed. "Si, perhaps I will visit him in Piombino. I seem to remember him wanting a picture of the Florentine lady. I will have to talk to him. In the meantime, father, see if you can work things out with the council. It is an impossible project. I must have out of it."

Chapter 47 – Piombino

That summer Ser Piero passed away at seventy-eight, leaving Leonardo nothing in his will. Following his father's advice, later that autumn, he traveled southwest toward the coast. He brought only a servant and his companion, Salai, with him.

"What about the wall, da Vinci?" Salai asked, more to irk him than out of curiosity. "The council will not like it that you have stopped work."

"Bah, they have their hunchback, Michelangelo, to fawn over. I have had enough of them."

"Why are you going to Piombino?" asked 'little-devil'.

"We are going for a holiday," answered the fifty-one-year-old artist. "There is someone there who may have a commission for me."

"But you already have one, two, unfinished, if I am not mistaken."

"Salai, will you please give me peace. I want to concentrate on what I am doing. I need to find the Medici."

"Is not your great patron, Cesare Borgia, here in the city? I am sure he has set up court in the castle."

"Ah, Salai, I see you are a wealth of information today, but it is not Borgia I wish to see."

"Aye, but he may want to see you. I am sure he will have some great thing for your military genius to do."

"Per favore, Salai, cease your babble. If I want information from you I will ask for it."

Salai lapsed into silence as their horses clip-clopped into the small fishing village of Piombino.

Someone looking for the great painter would have had no trouble finding him. He was dressed as flamboyantly as ever in an Arab burnoose and dusty, rose-colored, Catalan gown that only went to his knees. Rose stockings showed off the rest of his still muscular legs. A pink cap sat on his head.

Giuliano spotted him immediately from the porch of the Piombino de Medici villa. He was not alone. Niccolo Machiavelli had joined him earlier that afternoon.

"There is Master da Vinci," observed Giuliano pointing down toward the street.

"Yes, who can miss him? He stands out in a crowd," answered Machiavelli.

Sending a servant to fetch him, Giuliano and his guest went back inside to get out of the sun.

"Welcome, Master," said Giuliano when Leonardo and his entourage were shown into the villa's veranda. "I have been expecting you. Come, sit. Have some iced Chianti. You must be hot and exhausted after your trip. How are things in Mother Florence?"

"Fine, but si, it has been a hot, dry trip. Iced wine would be nice right now. Grazie. This is a surprise, Niccolo," said Leonardo looking at Machiavelli. "I did not expect to see you here, but than you are at home everywhere, excepting perhaps at Borgia's castle."

"That is so, my friend. I will no longer have anything to do with the man after what happen last year."

"This is a lovely villa," commented Leonardo. "Do you own it, Giuliano? I did not know you had property here."

"Yes, my grandfather, Cosimo, built this house," Giuliano answered. "It was one of his favorites. I hear you have been busy in the Palazzo della Signoria."

"Do not mention that name to me," replied the painter. "It has become a curse. The mural is in ruins and will never be finished."

"That is too bad," said Giuliano, "but now you will be free to return to Lisa Giocondo's painting."

Before the painter could answer, Machiavelli chimed in.

"I was hoping the Master could help us drain the swamps surrounding the castle here. They are an impediment to good commerce and good health."

"Are you sure you are not doing this for Borgia?" Giuliano inquired. "After all, he is the one holding court at the castle."

"No, he is an interloper," answered the Florentine statesman and philosopher. "He will soon be gone. This is for the city and the Republic of Pisa that rules it."

"Master," interrupted Giuliano. "You have already promised to paint the Giocondo portrait. It is mostly finished. Just a few more touches, a few weeks work, will complete it. It is only right that you do this before engaging in any new work. Especially something as time consuming as draining the Piombino swamps."

"Ah, yes, I almost forgot the lovely young mother, your lover once, if I am not mistaken."

"You are not mistaken that I love her, more than anything in the world, and I would give anything to have a picture of her."

"But is it not promised to Signore Giocondo, her husband?" the painter asked. "He is the one requesting the commission, is he not?"

"I will pay you a second commission to go back to work on it. I will double it."

The offer made the painter stop and think.

"It is early yet," said Leonardo. "I will come next March to Florence and finish the painting then. A second commission would be welcome. You and Francesco can fight over who gets the painting. I will work with Niccolo in the meantime, to drain his pesky swamps.

"Good," said Machiavelli. "Let us drink to it."

Chapter 48 – The Return

Spring had finally returned to Tuscany after a long, dreary winter. The budding leaves and flowers had little effect on Lisa's mood. It was 1507, four years after Leonardo had first come to paint her.

Nothing could dispel her gloom. She lived in the past with only the bitter sting of her memories to comfort her. She still pictured Giuliano as he had been when he was a teenager. For these were the memories she held closest, the intimate moments when they were in each other's arms.

She regretted there had been so few such moments, only enough to count with one hand, but they were what filled her life, not the things around her. She went through the day helping with the chores and taking care of the little ones, but there was no one behind her actions, only an empty shell.

She had not slept with her husband for almost two years. He had not said anything, although he was sorely disappointed. He understood, perhaps too well.

He had heard word from Leonardo, who said he would be back in Florence in the spring. Spring was here but there was no da Vinci. Francesco was about to inquire, when word came that the artist was back in the city and would be visiting them soon. He told Lisa.

"I heard word today that Master da Vinci is back in Florence and intends to continue with your painting."

"Who cares?" answered Lisa. "Not I. I care not where that awful man goes or what he does."

"Do you not want your picture finished?"

"It matters not a fig to me. I do not like it. It makes me look fat."

"It is not finished. Once he completes it, your beauty will be frozen for all time."

"You should have sued him."

"Do not be silly, dear. I knew he would come back."

"You are the one who said how unreliable he was. You were right. I do not have any faith in the man. He is just as liable to get your hopes up and then abandon you again. Hire another to finish the painting."

"I cannot do that, my dear. Then I would be the one being sued. Do not be so petulant, Lisa. Let him come and finish the painting."

"As you wish, husband, but I will not enjoy sitting for him. It no longer means anything to me."

Lisa's mood did not bode well for the enterprise, but Francesco looked up to heaven, made the sign-of-the-cross, and hoped for the best.

Leonardo appeared on the front doorstep of the Giocondo family villa the following morning. All his material was still in the attic room where it had been stored, along with the half-finished painting itself, under an oil-rag. To save time, since the background had already been finished, he continued the painting in the attic, hanging drapes to darken the room.

Lisa was less than pleased. As she was sitting in her pose, however, before painting, Leonardo addressed her.

"Our friend, Giuliano, sends his compliments. He told me to tell you that he longs to see you again, and if he cannot see you in the flesh, then to paint a portrait of you that will seem life-like. So here I am. That should make you smile a little."

And it did, with tears in her eyes. Giuliano was thinking of her. He longed for her. She finally remembered that this picture was for him. It was like heaven had opened and shined a light on her. It brought her to life. The transition was instantaneous. Suddenly, she was no longer morose, but radiant.

Da Vinci painted.

Lisa's emotions were so close to the surface that they cried out for the brush. This was the essence of Leonardo's genius, his style. He painted two-dimensional objects with perspective, giving them the appearance of three-dimensional objects. However, his paintings not only captured the outward appearance of the subject, but their inner feelings and thoughts as well. Lisa, with her honest, heartfelt emotions was an exceptional subject.

There was no set schedule for Leonardo's comings and goings. Sometimes he would come only for a short time, making a few dabs with the brush and leaving. Sometimes he would come and spend the whole day, late into the night, painting. He often came only for one day and did not return for several. Other times he would come for many days in a row.

Sometimes Lisa sat for him. Often, she would stand and watch the Master work, mesmerized by his stories and anecdotes. As before, jugglers, clowns, mimes, and musicians entertained her and kept her gay. This went on for several weeks.

As the days progressed, he added layer upon layer of paint, playing with shadow and light like a virtuoso pianist plays with scales. And with each layer, the picture came more and more to life.

The fine, delicate lines he added at the ends of the mouth were almost imperceptible, giving the impression the lips were smiling even though they were turned down. The eyes were rendered with such soft brush strokes they shone with a natural luster that made them truly windows into the soul.

The fleshy rose and pearly tints of the skin seemed not to be paint but real flesh. One could see the pulsing of the veins in the hollow of her throat. The nose, with its delicate pink nostrils, the mouth, where the lips merged with the skin tones of the face, all made it so real it looked like her image in a mirror.

Even the eyebrows were exquisite. Each hair appeared to spring from the skin, curving according to the pores and shape of the brow so naturally, each detail meticulously done. It is a pity they were lost to posterity, but at the time they made the picture come to life.

Still there was something missing, something elusive yet highly desired.

Chapter 49 – The Smile

One day during what would be the end of the sitting, unknown to everyone in Florence except da Vinci, Giuliano accompanied him to the Giocondo villa. He was disguised as one of the master's students, in an extravagant costume owned by Salai. It had a cowl that partially hid his face.

Acting as da Vinci's assistant, he carried the master's tools to the attic. Now he stood alone, unseen, behind a curtain hanging across a corner of the room. He was behind the artist, slightly to the left of twenty-eight-year-old Lisa, who sat facing them.

Slowly, imperceptibly, he began to pull the curtain aside. Leonardo was telling Lisa a humorous anecdote to entertain her and keep her spirits up while he painted. It was a story about when he, Giuliano, and Machiavelli were together with Borgia in Parvia, and was designed to make her smile, if not laugh.

When Lisa saw Giuliano emerge from behind the curtain, she thought it was a mirage and shook her head. When she opened her eyes again, he was still there. Leonardo, with his quick hands and dexterity, captured the moment in time - the sparkle in her eyes, the half-smile, half-smirk on her lips.

Lisa screamed and ran to her lover, clasping him to her like a cloak in a storm. Leonardo kept on painting as if nothing had happened, using his prodigious memory to continue working on the portrait, while the curtain was slowly closed. Behind it Giuliano and Lisa made passionate love.

Francesco was not home. He was being honored by the council for his cultural contribution to the city as a patron of the arts. The banquet was set up at Leonardo's request and presided over by his friend, Machiavelli, secretary of the Florentine Republic. He ensured the meeting would go until well after dinner, when Giuliano would presumably be gone.

Back in the attic of the villa, Giuliano tore the heavily-brocaded cloak from Lisa's body, while kissing her neck and shoulders. Ripping off her delicate, white bodice, he kissed her breasts passionately, thinking to himself how much nicer they were than the childlike bosoms Lucrezia was so proud of.

Lisa tore at Giuliano clothing as well, so that he was first bare-chested and then naked. His smooth buttocks and strong legs thrilled her. She kissed him as she guided him to her, his bare chest pressed against hers.

Slowly, a deep rapture enveloped them. Time stood still. The world and all its people disappeared. They floated on another plane, where only their love existed. Each moment, each kiss, each touch, was eternal bliss. They exploded together, simultaneously, in each other's arms.

The painter had long ago left. The sun had set. Yet still they lingered together lying arm in arm.

"It is getting late," said Giuliano. "I must go before Francesco returns."

"No, I know him," she answered. "He will stay out drinking and celebrating all night. It is a big tribute for him to be honored so."

"Yes, but he like I would not want to leave you alone for long. He will come running back to you to see the picture. I believe the Master has finished. He is leaving the city for Milan at the request of the French King, Louis."

"That cannot be," objected Lisa. "Surely the painting is not yet finished."

"Maybe not, but he has other obligations."

At that moment, Francesco entered the house and called for Lisa. She and her lover panicked and rapidly dressed. They could hear Francesco coming up the stairs to the attic. While Giuliano hid behind the curtain, Lisa went out to meet her husband.

"What is this?" stormed Francesco. "Where is the painting? It is gone!"

The painting and all the artist's equipment had disappeared. It was as if there had never been a painting. The silk merchant was shocked.

"The Master has left for Milan," answered Lisa, relating what Giuliano had told her. She hoped the missing painting would distract him from finding her lover.

"What? He cannot do that," objected her husband. "The painting was not finished. In any case, it belongs to me. How long ago did he leave?"

"Oh, several hours past," replied Lisa. "I was busy with the children and did not see him go."

"I will have him brought back in chains," vowed Francesco. "Where did you say he has gone?"

"To Milan. I am afraid that if you want to complain, you will have to complain to the king of France."

Francesco was beside himself. In a rage, he tore out of the house swearing. Giuliano slowly peeked from behind the curtain. Lisa ran to him and grabbing his hands, kissed them. He kissed her back on the lips and told her he would love her always.

He knew he must leave, for his life would be forfeit if he was discovered in the city, but he could not. Coming back to her time and again, he hugged and kissed her ardently.

Despite his fear, he could not tear himself from her. He clung to her like a frantic supplicant on his knees, his arms tight around her waist, his head pressed to her abdomen. Finally, the noise of horses in the courtyard outside forced him to flee out the back door. Ten minutes later he was on his horse outside the city walls, riding toward Rome.

Chapter 50 – A Memento

Things returned to normal in the Giocondo household. Since ser Piero, Leonardo's father, had died, Francesco had given up all hope of getting the painter to return the portrait of his wife. Since the commission had not been paid, he dropped the matter. He chalked it up to the eccentricities of artists, and went about his business. He had other things to celebrate. His wife had had another child. They named her Marietta.

The baby was born nine months to the day after the visit by Giuliano. Although Lisa had begun to sleep with her husband again soon after, she was sure the child was her lover's. She cherished the little girl like a gift from heaven, which it was. It immediately became her favorite. She gave the baby all her attention.

Francesco was happy to be back in Lisa's bed and delighted with the new baby girl. He was surprised it had happened, since even when sleeping together they hardly had intercourse, and that barely successful at best. He wondered about it. It was as if Lisa had orchestrated the whole thing, but he did not question the gift, as it seemed to change Lisa for the better.

She now smiled every day, all day, at least at first. As the child grew older, she looked more and more like a miniature version of her mother, with raven hair, rosy cheeks, pretty brown eyes, and a dainty nose. She smiled back into her mother's eyes like a little mirror. And every time she saw that smile Lisa thought of Giuliano and his precious gift to her. Her greatest fear was that the child would be taken from her like her other one was, but after the years passed without a whisper of grief, she soon forgot the fear entirely.

With the passing of the years, however, her memory of Giuliano began to fade. She had not forgotten his face, but it had lost substance. She no longer saw it clearly in her mind's eye. He became only a shadow, and over time, even that disappeared. The faint hues of life that her memory had given her were gone.

The long sundering had wasted away even the power of imagining. It left her despondent and emotionless, bereft of tears and smiles, only empty boredom. Only her child, Marietta, gave her any joy and even that was fading with the bitter hope of ever seeing her lover again. She had only a past she could not remember, and no hope in a future she would never have. Only never-ending loneliness filled her days.

Francesco did his best to meet the growing sadness of his wife, buying her more fine clothes that she never wore; taking her to expensive banquets she would not partake of. He lamented that he never got the painting, which might have relieved some of her pain. He wondered if someone else had gotten it and cursed the one he thought of. But he did not pursue the matter, which he thought of as a tangle of worms.

There were moments when her pain was held in abeyance, as she played with, or slept with, or bathed her little girl, but these moments were becoming more infrequent and tainted with a vague longing, as if something were out of joint.

Francesco and Lisa took holidays by the sea and traveled to other places, like Pisa, Ravenna, and Rome, but nothing changed the blank look of sadness on her face as she gazed off into a distance only she could see. Over the years her separation from Giuliano became like a millstone around her neck, weighing her down.

The separation was weighing on Giuliano, too, although he tried to hide it from those around him. He was in Rome, biding his time, until the Holy Alliance against the French was strong enough to eject them from the country. Charles VIII was ill and there was hope that the French grip on Milan would loosen. Giuliano and others increased their exertions in this direction, but it did not distract the Medici from his obsession.

He had sent a letter to da Vinci asking about the painting but had gotten no reply. The artist, who was still in Milan, did not bother to answer. Giuliano hardly noticed he was so busy.

His brother, Giovanni, was now a cardinal and thought of as a likely successor of the Pope. A worldly man, it was not so much his saintliness, which was questionable, as his good judgment and ability to make money. It allowed him to get things done that others could not and solve problems many thought unsolvable.

Giuliano's many responsibilities enabled him to ignore the pain and hold despair at bay, but it left him drained of energy. He saw no end to his loneliness. He allowed himself only three hours sleep each night, from 1:00 am until 4:00. He was so exhausted that he hardly noticed how tired he was. He was serving a cause - the recovery of his home and city, Florence, but he suffered from the loss of Lisa, his love.

Always one to control his temper, his emotions had grown hard and brittle. His sensibilities were getting out of hand. He snapped completely every now and then without warning. He found himself apologizing for his outbursts more and more often.

With no answer other than to tighten his control on his feelings and harden his heart, he sank deeper into melancholy. The protective shield he had built around himself, which had worked at first to help him carry on, now sapped him of life and joy, leaving him nothing but a bare, empty, freezing-numb shell.

He had few delusions left and fatigue had robbed him of even these. Yet he went on fighting, hardly eating or sleeping, like one of the mechanical automatons Master da Vinci made to entertain the people at court, an empty clockwork machine with no hope and no soul.

"Oh, if I only had her picture," he lamented to Giovanni one evening. "Then I could stand being without her. Why does not da Vinci answer my letters? Do I have to go to Milan myself to see it?"

"That would not be a bad idea," replied his brother.

"But the French are there. They would not abide it."

"Si," answered his brother. "You will have to go at the head of an army and drive them out once I am Pope."

"I only hope I can last that long," replied Giuliano.

Chapter 51 – Milan

Leonardo had left Florence in early 1507 and gone back to Milan at the invitation of the royal governor, Charles d'Ambrose. He packed all his possessions in chests and trunks, including the Giocondo painting, and loaded them onto several mules. He and his students, Salai and Melzi, then traveled along the Italian coast of the Ligurian Sea to Genoa. Next, they crossed the Alps to France going by way of the Montgenevre Valley. There, they spent several days resting.

Traveling further east to Grenoble, they spent some weeks in a monastery on a hill as a guest of the monks, courtesy of Giuliano's brother the Cardinal. They then traveled north to Lyon where the painter had many friends but no commissions. Finally, after another month, they turned southeast to head back over the Alps to Milan, where d'Ambrose greeted them with open arms.

The trip took three months, which gave Leonardo plenty of time to gauge the attitude of the French, which appeared sincere. By late May he had reached his destination.

By the end of 1508 he was living in a parish church courtesy of the governor. Da Vinci was hired as an engineer and scientist and given a generous and regular stipend. Never one to look back, but to always have his sights on what lay ahead, he had all but forgotten about Lisa's portrait.

"I cannot bear the sight of a paint brush," he said, when asked to paint something by his patron, d'Ambrose.

He would much rather spend his nights dissecting corpses and his days designing fortresses and machines of war. Fascinated with the things of nature, he studied light, sight, aerodynamics, the formation of clouds, the color of the sky, the heart and arteries, birth and death, and everything in between. Though not a Christian in his belief, he was a child of God, a believer in man as witness to God's creation, which he gave glory to. The more he learned, the closer he felt to the Creator.

Leonardo kept himself busy day and night with new projects and inventions. Never slacking in his thirst for knowledge and truth, he was tireless in his efforts to learn all and everything he could. And in time, everything he would learn would go into his painting of the Florentine lady, Mona Lisa. For now, however, it lay untouched in a trunk.

The seasons changed, projects came and went, Leonardo marked the days as they turned into weeks and then months and years. In the spring of 1509, the French king, Charles VIII visited Milan to great celebrations.

There were processions and pageants, festivals and passion plays, all of which required the Master's talents. Stages had to be set, fireworks planned, scenery and backdrops designed.

Leonardo spent many hours creating one of his mechanical lions, which jumped and opened its mouth. It was the sensation of the festivities, a marvel to behold. It would be the last time the king would visit Milan. He died soon after.

Through all this period, Leonardo had taken his time unpacking. He had taken in many more books and written many more notes, while his paintings gathered dust sitting in trunks and chests.

It was around this time that da Vinci, looking for a specific notebook, came across the Giocondo portrait. He took it out of the trunk and placed it on a table, leaning it against the wall, where the soft light from a high window played on it. He stood and stared at the painting for the longest time, not moving.

Time stood still. It was as if he was lost in a trance. He forgot himself, and although he had not fallen asleep, became suddenly aware. The sun, which had been shining through the east-facing window, now gently glowed in a western-facing one. A late-day yellow light splayed onto the floor. Where had the time gone?

No thoughts had passed his mind, at least none he could remember, only the image, which stayed with him, and a feeling of elation. It was as if he had found something he had lost, like God. He'd had many lovers in his long life, pretty boys and young, well-formed men, but had he loved? Now he could not remember.

Yes, he loved Melzi like a son and treated him as such, but not as a lover. Salai had been the closest he came to loving, but few could love such an impish, sour boy. Now, staring at the painting of Lisa, he felt he had finally found love, not the girl, but the painting itself.

As the light changed to dusk, the artist lit a lamp, then walked back and forth in front of the painting, viewing it from different angles, studying the eyes – which seemed to follow him - the pretty nose, the mysterious mouth, the smooth neck, the fine hands, in turn. He stopped and stared at a tiny spot, and then another, studying each point intently, memorizing each inch of the canvas.

He called to his companion.

"Salai, mix my paints, per favore."

"Are you sure, Master?" his young friend asked. "I thought you did not want to touch a paint brush."

"Please, Salai, just do it," said Leonardo. He did not take his gaze off the canvas.

The sun had slipped over the lip of the mountains, dabbing a delicate amber hue on the dark wood panel. The rest of the room was in shadow. Taking his brush, he applied light strokes of pink on Lisa's dark robe. He would come back to the painting often over the rest of his life to lay more delicate, almost insubstantial layers of oil, until he had it just the way he wanted - perfect.

Chapter 52 – Giuliano's Dream

That evening, many miles away in Rome, a light rain bathed the streets and washed the dirt of the day away. As the clouds vanished, the stars appeared in the firmament one by one, undiminished by any moon. As tired as Giuliano was, he doubted he could sleep. His mind was abuzz with conversations he'd had during the day and decisions he'd have to make on the morrow. To put his mind to rest he thought about Lisa and the last time he had seen her.

He pictured in his mind how she had appeared, first, in her clothing and how it hung on her, how it showed her neck and bosoms, how her eyes had shown, how her lips smiled. When he had her firm in his memory, he imagined touching her and feeling her, her neck bones, her ribs, her breasts, her stomach. And as he imagined each body part, he pictured kissing and fondling it. He soon became aroused but instead of pleasuring himself, he kept the image in his mind and soon fell asleep.

He was not one to remember his dreams. Possibly it was because his sleep was so short. Was it that he had no dreams? Or did he just not remember? This night, however, he would recall. The memory of that dream would be with him every waking moment for the rest of his life.

He seemed lost and looking for something. He was in a busy street of some city, surrounded by people going to and fro to their appointed rounds. Everyone was in a costume. Although he didn't recognize the city, he assumed it was Florence. This gave his search a purpose.

Lisa was in Florence. He was determined to find her. But where could she be? Nothing around him was familiar. For all he knew he might not be in Florence at all, but he wished it to be so. After all, it was his dream. He kept searching for her.

He tried to reason it out. She lived near the wall, so in his dream he started looking for a wall. But as he searched up one street and down another, he became more and more convinced that she was just ahead of him, running away.

He picked up his pace. No longer searching, he was trying to catch her. Faster and faster he ran, hungering for that which was just out of reach, and not yet in sight. Then he saw the hem of a robe flit around a corner. He tore after it only to see it disappear around a another.

The elusive robe kept just out of reach, although he could see it plainly now. Was that Lisa running from him? It had to be. Who else could it be? A flash of skin, a splash of color, he was getting closer. He was almost upon her now. He could smell her hair. Arriving at the last corner just as her image disappeared around it he reached out and grabbed her arm, holding it tight.

It was Lisa!

He had her in his arms. Her scent was fresh and unmistakable. Her eyes looked at him with desire. Her lips parted. He kissed them. It was bliss. It was real. He felt all the pleasure that having her in his arms had ever given him. It was no longer a dream. He was lost in oblivion, an eternity in the moment.

Giuliano woke suddenly, still feeling her next to him, her delectable odor still in his nostrils, the taste of her still on his lips.

He did not want to wake up, and tried to fall back asleep into his dream. When that failed, he laid there and relived the dream in his imagination, until that too faded and he pulled himself out of the bed.

He had wet himself during the night. It was not urine.

Rather than invigorating him and giving him joy, the dream put him in a sour mood. It made him miss her even more. He was sick that he could not get back into it. His love was further away than ever. He despaired of ever seeing her again, let alone making love to her.

He realized then that it wasn't her he had pictured that evening, but her portrait. It stood out in his memory even after her real image had faded. Her portrait was the only thing that tied her to him. If only he had her picture, it would be like having her in the flesh. He had to have it. He realized that he could not live without it.

Chapter 53 – The Letter

The year was 1512. Francesco came home early to tell Lisa the news.

"Lisa, I have been elected to the Signoria. It is a very great honor. I am now in the governing body of our great city."

"Congratulations, my husband. I am very proud of you. We should celebrate."

"We have something even greater to celebrate," he continued excitedly. "The French have been driven from Milan. It is a great day. The Holy League is expanding. Soon, hopefully, all the foreigners will be driven out of Italy and we can have our land back."

"They will be back," replied Lisa with pessimism. She did not much care who invaded what.

"Perhaps da Vinci will come back to Florence now that his protectors are gone and bring back your picture."

"Have you heard from the Master?" she asked.

"No, he does not bother to respond to my entreaties, and now that his father is gone, I have no one to intercede for us. Perhaps I will write to Giuliano de Medici. He might be able to help."

"Giuliano? You know where he is?"

"Yes, he is in Rome with his brother, the Cardinal."

Lisa pretended not to care, but the mention of her lover's name made her shake with nervous energy. Her breathing became rapid. Her face flushed. She tried not to show her agitation.

"Ludovico Sforza's brother, the young Maximilian, is the Duke of Milan now," he told Lisa. "I hope his Swiss mercenaries can protect him."

Lisa said nothing. She was thinking of Giuliano in Rome and how she longed to see him.

"How is Marietta doing?" Francesco asked of their youngest daughter. "She will be five in a few days. She is getting to look more and more like you every day. Perhaps we should have a party for her."

"That would be nice," replied his wife.

"You spend so much time with her. You neglect the other children."

"She is young and needs me more."

"Why are you so attached to her?" asked Francesco.

"She reminds me of little Piera who we lost," Lisa answered. "It is like she has come back in Marietta."

"Well, you must wean her of you, or she will become too dependent."

"There is no such thing as a child being too close to her mother."

"Then perhaps you can explain this," he said, taking a letter from his pouch.

"What is it?" she asked.

"A letter I found in your drawer."

"What are you doing in my drawer? Those are my private possessions."

"We are man and wife. We must have no secrets from each other."

"It is not polite to go through my things."

"What is it?" demanded her husband.

"As you said, it is a letter. What of it?"

"Since when do you get letters from other men?"

"Who says it is from a man?"

"It is a declaration of love!" Francesco yelled.

Lisa was silent.

"And this?" he continued, taking from the pages a lock of dark hair.

"Who is it from?" she asked feigning innocence. "I know nothing about this letter you say you found."

"It is from Giuliano."

"No," she answered, grabbing the paper from his hand.

Of course it was from Giuliano, sent to her soon after they last saw each other. She pretended to read it as if for the first time.

"Oh," she said, feigning amusement. "This is from when we were children. I had forgotten I had it."

"Do not lie to me, Lisa. You have been a good wife but perhaps you have been only acting. You still love this Medici?"

"No, I love you, my husband. This is just a childhood fancy, nothing more, a memento of my youth. It means nothing."

"Sometimes I think the whole idea of a portrait was Giuliano's idea. He is the one who talked to ser Piero so that his son would paint your picture. No wonder it was never delivered. This Medici has it. As a matter of fact, I half suspect he is the real father of your precious child."

"No!" Lisa said loudly in protest. "How can you say such a thing? Marietta is your child, Francesco."

"I wonder. I wish I could be sure. I curse the day that painter came into our lives. The Medici is behind all this. It is just like those treacherous bankers to do such a thing. Soon his brother will be pope. Then where will we be?"

"You talk crazy, Francesco. It is not so. This is just an old letter from an old friend, who I have not seen in many years. I was but fourteen, since before we were married."

"How come I have not found it sooner?"

"You must not have looked. You trusted me once," said Lisa.

"I will not make that mistake again," he said, storming out of the room.

Lisa was shaken by the exchange. She held the letter close to her heart and cried silently. Soon little Marietta came into the room to have her hair curled.

Lisa picked up the little girl and hugged her tightly.

"You are my precious angel," she said holding the child upright before her. "You mean everything to me."

"I am your angel," the little girl repeated. "I am going to be beautiful like you."

"Yes, you are. You will be the most beautiful girl in all of Florence. We will have to have a picture painted of you."

Chapter 54 – Wandering

"We must leave Milano," said sixty-year-old Leonardo to his companions. "Maximilian, Massimiliano, they call him, is still young. Unlike his father, Ludovico, he does not appreciate us and has nothing for me."

"But where will we go, Maestro?" asked Salai.

"I do not know but we cannot stay here. Not only are there no commissions, but it is not safe with all the Swiss troops loafing around. They are all bullies and looking for trouble. Load my trunks and the chests. We will ride tonight."

"But I have many things that must be packed," objected Salai. "All my beautiful clothes and jewels."

"Leave the clothes, Salai. I will buy you new ones," Leonardo said.

The artist packed the Giocondo painting himself, which he had been working on intermittently for the past year.

Leonardo and his two companions left the city that evening.

Wandering the countryside around Milan for several days, Leonardo sought news of possible destinations and patrons. Given the state of affairs in the city and surrounding area, however, there was little in the form of prospects.

As they sat around the fire one evening, roasting chestnuts for their supper, Francesco Melzi, his heir and protégé, spoke.

"My family's home is not far from here," he told them. They were twenty miles outside of Milan. "We could go there. My parents will be happy to see us. I am sure they would put us up until you can find a patron."

An hour later they were at the Melzi villa in Vaprio overlooking the Adda. As Francesco had promised, his family welcomed them open-heartedly. They had their first real meal in days.

"I understand that the French royal governor was you friend," said the elder Melzi, a captain in the Milanese militia and a civil engineer by trade. "Where are you going, Maestro, now he is gone?"

"It is uncertain," answered da Vinci. "Everything is in flux since the French have left. Perhaps Rome."

"Would not the new duke, Maximilian, hire you? I imagine he would have good need for your military genius, if not your skill as an artist."

"He is but a youth, not yet twenty. He has not an appreciation for the fine arts. Although he is not unpleasant to look at, with his long, golden hair and pretty, girlish face, I find nothing in him that would inspire admiration. He seems rather simple to me."

"Not so simple that he could not win back the city of his father."

"Si, poor Lodovicio, to spend his dying days in a dark, dank prison. I thought it prudent to absent myself from Milan, in any case."

"Si, it was probably a wise decision. I do not know yet how my militia will fare. The duke seems to favor the Swiss."

"Those blood-thirsty mercenaries are a bane to mankind," commented da Vinci.

"My son says you have painted the most wonderful picture," said the elder Melzi, changing the subject. "Do you have it with you? I was wondering if you would grace us by showing it to us."

"I have many paintings," replied da Vinci. "Do you have one in particular in mind?"

Melzi looked at his son.

"Francesco?" he said

"I think he means the Giocondo portrait," answered his son. "I may have mentioned it in a letter."

"Yes, the Florentine lady, I think you said," replied his father.

"It is in one of the trunks," Leonardo told them. "Perhaps Salai will retrieve it for us."

"I have already taken it out and hung it on the wall of your bedroom as you asked, Maestro," said his companion and sometime student.

"Ah, Salai, good man. If you would be so kind, Signore Melzi, to join me in the room you have so generously assigned me, I can show it to you now."

They all went up to the second-floor apartment, which looked out over the Adda Valley. The picture hung opposite the west window. The waning light of the day illuminated it in a fine yellow haze. Only two feet, six inches by one foot, nine, the picture had become Leonardo's favorite. Not only did he take it everywhere with him, but he worked on it often and looked at it constantly.

Francesco's father stared at it in awe.

"Master, I have never seen such a painting. You have brought this lady to life. The texture of the robe is so rich as to be real. The madam's eyes shine with a luster as if alive. They appear to smile. Dear God, Master, you have captured that ineffable emotion that lies beyond words. You have looked into this person's soul and painted it. It is astounding."

Leonardo said nothing, nor did he acknowledge the compliment. Although no one else could tell, he knew the work was not yet complete. It would take many more years to uncover its true perfection.

"Oh, that I could have such a painting," said his host.

"Maybe Francesco will make a copy for you," suggested Leonardo, "if we are here long enough."

"Please, you may stay as long as you like," said the senior Melzi. "Francesco?"

"Father, I am afraid I have not yet the skill to do this painting justice. I have much to learn before I could copy such a picture. It has all of the master's scientific knowledge, built up from years of study, as well as all he knows of God and man, which is infinite."

"You give me too much credit, my dear apprentice," said Leonardo. "You must aim high and do your best. Who knows what you might accomplish. We will see."

Leonardo ended up spending almost a year at the Melzi villa, designing plans for its improvement and the enlargement of the living quarters. He also spent many hours walking in the nearby hills, sketching dramatic pictures of the landscape. In his spare time, he dissected animals caught in the area for his anatomic studies.

All through this time, the Mona Lisa painting hung in his room. It was the first thing he saw on waking in the morning and the last thing he gazed on at night. It fired his dreams and kindled his imagination. And every so often, when the mood took him, he dabbed more oil on the panel of poplar wood in fine, delicate strokes.

Chapter 55 – Homecoming

Unknown to Leonardo and his host, Pope Julius II had died. The year was 1513. A new Pope had been elected, none other than Giuliano's brother, Giovanni de Medici. He took the name, Pope Leo X. Together with the secular power of the Vatican and the support of the Spanish, the longed-for recovery of Florence became a reality.

Giovanni had made his brother, Giuliano, commander and chief of the papal army. He could not wait to go home and reclaim his rightful place as ruler. Soon after that, the Republic of Florence collapsed, and its leaders were driven into exile. Giuliano de Medici entered the city triumphantly after twenty years an outcast. He had changed greatly in those years.

Disillusioned by failure, saddened by loneliness, ill with a slowly progressing disease, he was not the man he used to be. Restless with inactivity, his melancholy had grown, threatening to engulf him. A leaden heart beat a dirge to life, a life of debauchery and bitterness. Only one thing gladdened his days, the thought of seeing Lisa again, if not her, at least her portrait. The first thing he did after entering the city was visit the Gioconda villa.

He had heard that Francesco, Lisa's husband, had been imprisoned in the last days of the Republic for his support of the Medici's return. For this reason, he had planned to have him released, but not until he had seen Lisa.

She was aware he was coming but not sure when he would arrive. With her husband in prison and her busy with their five children, she had little time to keep up with events. At thirty-five, the same age as Giuliano, she was still pretty if a little plump. Her eyes still sparkled, the smile still played on her lips when she thought of her lover. She loved her husband but thought of Giuliano. These musings were interrupted by a knock on the door.

"You have a visitor, Mistress," the servant announced. Without changing from her peasant blouse and rough hewn gown, she went to see who it was.

"Giuliano!" she said on seeing him. "You have come. I have waited so long."

"Buongiorno amore mio," he replied. "I have missed you."

"And I you, please come in and sit. Can I get you anything?"

"No, I have all I need on seeing you."

"Francesco, my husband, is in prison. I have been all alone here since last year."

"I know. I am having him released but first I wanted to see you."

"Thank you, my Lord."

"You do not have to be formal with me, my love."

Lisa was struck by how old Giuliano looked. He was haggard and gray. He seemed feeble and moved slowly, coughing often, but his dark eyes still shown bright when he looked at her and his hands were still as beautiful as ever. She longed for them to touch her but said nothing.

"All Florence rejoices in your return, as do I," she told him. "I have dreamed of this moment."

"As have I, my dearest," he replied.

They sat in silence, staring into each other's eyes. She wanted to run to him and fling herself into his arms like she had in the field of wildflowers. He wanted to crush her in his embrace like he did the last time they had met. He only asked how she was faring. She replied that she was well, considering the situation, and asked if he would like to see the garden.

She brought him to the rear of the villa, where a small enclosure of stone and evergreen hedges lay. Boxwood and cypress trees were interspersed with juniper and rosemary bushes. Geranium and white lilies lined the edge of the space and walkways. He plucked one and put it in her hair. They sat on a stone bench in the middle of the garden.

"I have missed you so," Lisa said when they were alone.

"And I you," he answered.

"Will you be staying here in Florence?"

"I am commander of the Pope, my brother's, troops. I go where he needs me."

Lisa did not reply but sat looking into his eyes.

"I love you Lisa, more than anything," he said. "I have only wanted to die since I could not be with you. It is only the hope that I would see you again that kept me from killing myself."

"No, my dearest, do not talk like that. You have so much to live for."

"I have nothing to live for if I cannot have you. Come away with me."

"I remember when you first asked me that. It was so long ago. I could not go with you then because of my family."

"And now? Can you come away with me now?"

"Please, do not ask me that. I have my own family to take care of now."

"Yes, I see. The little ones, they are lovely," he said. "If you will not come with me, then I must know, where is the painting Master Leonardo did of you? I must see it."

"I do not know," she replied. "It was never delivered to us. My husband thought that you might have it."

"No, not I, though I wish it were so. It must still be with the Master. I will ask about it next time I see him."

"He is in Milan, I believe," she said. "Francesco has asked about it, but the artist never replied. He was going to ask you to help. Now he needs more help."

"I must see Leonardo. I want him to come to Rome with me, but first we must set Francesco free."

At that moment, six-year-old Marietta came into the backyard.

"Mommy, Matilda asked me if the man will stay for dinner."

"Will you stay, Giuliano?" she asked.

"No, I cannot," he answered. "I have much to attend to."

"Go tell Matilda he will not be staying," Lisa told her little girl.

"The little one is beautiful. What is her name?"

"She is called Marietta," said Lisa. "She is yours."

"What? Mine?" replied Giuliano, not sure he had heard her correctly.

"She is your child, Giuliano. From the last time we were together."

He stood up and looked after the little girl, who had left the enclosure.

"Mine? She is a darling. Why did you not tell me sooner? Come, take her and come away with me. All my dreams would be answered. I could die a happy man."

"No, my dearest, I cannot go with you. You must go on and live for us, with us in your heart."

"Oh, my heart is broken, that the one I love and my own child must live with another. Please, say it is not so. I cannot stand this torture."

He knelt at her feet, tears streaming down his cheeks. She leaned toward him and caressed them from his face, kissing him. He rose, and embracing her, kissed her back. He held her with the same intensity she remembered, and kissed her with the passion he'd had when they were teenagers. Closing her eyes, she saw him as he once was, young and strong. His kisses were so forceful that she almost swooned.

"You must come away with me," he said again. "I cannot live without you."

"You must, Giuliano. You must go on. I must know you are well and happy, or my life is forlorn. We must love each other from afar."

"Oh, if only I had your picture. Then I could pretend you are with me. Then I could remember you as you are."

Their kisses were becoming more frenzied. His hands were all over her, pulling at her clothes. She stopped him, taking his hands in hers and kissing them.

"No, my love, we cannot. The little one may come back."

"Then I must go. I cannot stand to be close to you like this and not have you. I will take you by force if I stay."

"No, Giuliano, if you love me do not torture me so. Be strong. Be my friend but not my lover."

"But I am your lover. I love you more than all things. I must have you or I will die."

They were both crying now, tears streaming down their faces. He started to cough.

"Do not despair," she said. "Our love is eternal. You will always be first in my heart. It is your love that keeps me going. It fills me with joy, knowing we have been close and have loved. Our child is witness to our love, even though no one must ever know."

"No," he said between sobs and fits of coughing. "I am tired of living without you. I am tired of waking up alone, of seeing you with another. Take pity on me. What is life without love but empty and forlorn? Seeing all that I have lost, my love unfulfilled, is like a poison to my heart. It eats my soul, a futile hope without peace or solace. Must I go on and play my part alone? No, I would die for you if it would mean the end of my pain."

"No, Giuliano, you must live for your child and for me. Remember us."

'No, I must forget you if I cannot have you."

With that, he kissed her hand and left the villa. She heard his horse's hooves disappear down the cobbled road.

That night, Francesco returned from prison half-starved and beaten but glad to be home. She bathed and fed him but did not tell him of her visitor.

Chapter 56 – To Rome

In September of that same year, Giuliano, learning that Leonardo was in Vaprio, sent word to him to join him in Florence. The artist arrived a few weeks later and met his new patron at the Medici villa.

Giuliano had not resigned himself to life without Lisa, but was resolved to bide his time and seek other opportunities to win her. Little did he know he had not much time left.

"I have work for you in Rome, Master," Giuliano told da Vinci when they met. "We can go together. I will be like a brother to you."

Leonardo was flattered and looked forward to working for the Medici, although it was uncertain exactly what he would be doing.

"Do you have the painting?" Giuliano asked.

"What painting do you refer?" answered Leonardo. "I have several I am working on."

"Why, the Giocondo portrait, of course," Giuliano replied.

"Ah, that one. Yes, it is in my trunks with the others."

"I must see it. I must have it."

"It is not finished. I am still working on it."

"Still, after all this time?"

"Yes, it will be my masterpiece. I will show it to you when we are in Rome."

They left the next day, with Giuliano accompanying the artist, Francesco Melzi, and Salai, along with a new student and a servant. They arrived in Rome a few days later.

Leonardo and his entourage stayed in the Belvedere apartments at the Vatican, near the Papal palace. It had been repaired and renovated just for him. New furniture had also been installed and a studio added.

Giuliano helped him unpack and placed Lisa's portrait on an easel in the new studio for all to see. He came each day to sit and stare at it, much to Leonardo's chagrin.

The Master was not happy. Michelangelo was there, fresh from painting the ceiling of the Sistine Chapel, as well as Raphael, the Pope's favorite.

Leonardo was no longer in fashion, his reputation eclipsed by his younger rivals He felt out of place, an unhappy old man whose time had passed. Not being of a competitive nature, and not one to curry favor, he was elbowed aside by fast-talking charlatans with less talent,

179

and outmaneuvered by the younger men. Because of this, he was unable to carve out a place for himself at court or win a commission.

He occupied his time building fire-mirrors and complaining bitterly about the German assistants that Giuliano had hired for him. The thirty-three ducats that his patron paid him each month was not much when compared to the huge sums his rivals were getting.

Only sixty-one, the artist appeared much older. His long white beard made him look ancient. His eyesight was going and he was ill, complaining of various ailments and pains.

The new pope ignored him, and even though Giuliano did all he could for him, Leonardo was beginning to doubt the wisdom of moving to Rome. The only joy he got was working on the Lisa portrait, which he did on rainy, overcast days and evenings, when his protector was away, for otherwise, the Medici hogged the painting for himself.

Giuliano looked at it often, gazing on it as he had gazed at Lisa, looking into her eyes. If he stared at it long enough it became real to him, Lisa in the flesh, smiling at him. He could almost hear her breathing.

The year went by slowly for both of them. Giuliano's sickness progressed steadily. His eyes grew sunken. He coughed more often and spoke of suicide as if it were a lover. None of this helped Leonardo's mood. Even Giuliano's brother, the Pope, took notice.

"What is wrong with you, my brother," asked Giovanni, now Pope Leo X, one day toward the end of the year. "You wander the streets like a homeless person. You never smile and spend all your time staring at that woman's picture. Are you still pining over that girl after all this time?"

"I love her."

"But she is married to another and has been so for the past twenty years. You must get over it," said the Pope. "God has given us the papacy, let us enjoy it."

"I cannot," replied Giuliano. "I have nothing to live for."

"You must. I have arranged a marriage for you. You must get on with your life. The Duke of Savoy has a daughter. You are to marry her. It is important to strengthen the alliance."

Giuliano said nothing.

Where Giuliano was thin and tired of life, his brother, the Pope, was plump and fond of good living. Though not known for his piety, Leo X was well-read and traveled extensively. He handled papal affairs with moderation and wisdom. He encouraged the arts and attracted many of the best artists to the Eternal City. However, he ignored perhaps the greatest of them, the old master da Vinci.

"I am thinking of going back to Florence," Leonardo told his patron one day. "I am not wanted here."

"That is not so," answered Giuliano. "I want you here. I need you."

"For what? You have not given me a commission. You have me playing with fire-mirrors."

"They may be of use one day if you perfect them," the Medici insisted. "They could be the difference between victory or defeat if war breaks out again. The French are still at our doors."

"You have given me fools as assistants," answered da Vinci. "They are more of an obstacle than a help. You do not need me."

"You say I have given you no commissions. What about the one I gave you many years ago? Give me the painting of Lisa. I will pay you handsomely for it."

Leonardo said nothing for a time.

"It is for her husband," he finally replied. "It is promised to him."

"Then why do you not give it to him? Why do you hold on to it? I asked you to paint it long before your father offered it to him. It is mine. Please, Master, give me the painting. I need it to go on. Without it I am nothing."

"I hear you are to be married at the head of the year. How would that look? What would your new bride say?"

"She will have no say in the matter, just as I have no say in marrying her. It is my brother, the Pope's wish, not mine."

"And what does his Eminence say about it? Does he want you to have it?"

"He will not care as long as I do as he says."

"It is not finished," said da Vinci. "I have more to do."

"You have been painting it for twelve years! What more is there to do?"

"Much," Leonardo replied, "a lifetime more."

Giuliano could not get the painting from him, even though he begged.

Chapter 57 – Giuliano Marries

The New Year, 1515, arrived with much fanfare. Giuliano finally bowed to his brother's wishes and married Philiberta of Savoy. At about the same time, the French king, Louis XII, died and was succeeded by his young cousin and son-in-law, Francis, crowned the First.

The nineteen-year-old king was a giant of a man at six feet tall, with massive shoulders and bulging eyes. Everything about him was big, his nose and crimson lips, as well as his ambition. Before the crown was on his head, he set his eyes on Milan, which he soon took possession of after a brief battle.

Leonardo met him a few months later at the peace talks in Bologna, where Pope Leo X ate crow for backing the wrong horse in the brief war. The artist was as impressed with the warrior king as were most people. Francis was not only impressive to look on, but friendly and magnanimous, with an infectious personality. The king evidently thought the same of Leonardo, for he asked him to go back to France with him.

The artist won the king over with a mechanical lion he built with a spring-powered, clockwork motor. It allowed it to walk several paces then open its mouth to release a flock of fleur-de-lis. Still, Leonardo did not abandon his patron, Giuliano, immediately, but stayed with him in Rome, where he and his new wife were residing before going to Nemours to live.

Giuliano's health had deteriorated badly, slowly but surely, with the insidious disease hiding in his breast. His new wife was young and plain, an uninspiring fifteen-year-old who knew nothing of life. She would have been intelligent if given half a chance but as a woman, even a high-born one, she had been dominated by her father and his court, deprived of every opportunity to know about life, hidden and protected as a house cat.

She was not pleased with the thirty-six-year-old husband who was forced on her. Her heart sank when she first set eyes on him. He was but a pale comparison to the vibrant, captivating man she had been promised. Giuliano felt much the same toward her.

"Oh, that I could have married Lisa," Giuliano lamented to his brother, the Pope.

"Your new wife is the Duchess of Nemours," answered Giovanni. "You will be Duke. What is the problem?"

"I care not about being Duke," answered Giuliano. "The girl is not pretty. Nor does she like me, to judge from the utter look of contempt on her thin face when we met. She is boring and unaffectionate."

"Give her time," advised the Pope. "She will warm to you, I am sure. The important thing is her tie to the new French King. She is his aunt, although she is four years his junior. It will be a very beneficial relationship. I had to give much to win her hand for you. Do not let me down, Giuliano."

"Do not worry, your Eminence. I will do my duty, but I will not be happy."

"So, you are not happy. You were not happy before. What difference does it make?"

"Life is so cruel," lamented Giuliano. "What is the meaning of it? A monotonous series of never-ending days, I would be done with it. Death is so sweet if it ends the tedium of my existence. I dream of it. I long for it. If I cannot have my Lisa, I would have nothing. Let me lie in the arms of my mistress dead and cold, a lifeless statue for her to gaze on and weep for. Only then will I be satisfied."

"Do not be so morbid, Giuliano. Suicide is a mortal sin. Even to think about it is against God's will. Do not mock the Lord with your gloomy song. Your future is ahead of you, and a glorious future it will be if you follow the path chosen for you. Do it for your city, Florence. Do it for my city, Rome. Do it for Italy. You will live forever in people's hearts, but you must be brave and sacrifice your happiness for your land. Who knows, you may grow to love your wife and she you with time."

"I will never love another but Lisa. I will love her until the day I die, which I hope is soon."

"Ah, Giuliano, you are a sentimental fool. You make yourself miserable over a girl you knew when you were both children. She is married. Get over it. It is finished."

"I will never get over it," answered Giuliano.

"Maybe not but you can be sure she is over you."

"How can you say that? How can you know?"

"She has had five children with her husband. She is not thinking about you."

"That is not so. It is my child she had last."

"What? What are you saying, Giuliano?"

183

"Nothing, I have said too much already."

"Do not say such a thing again, even if you are fooling. Do you want to ruin everything?"

"No one will ever know."

"Let us hope not. I assume you are telling a joke, trying to upset me. I do not believe you, in any case. Now go to your young bride and give her a child, not the one in your imagination, but a real one. It may be king one day. Can you imagine, a Medici on the throne of France? Our father, Lorenzo, would smile down on us with pride."

"Perhaps on you, but not me, for I have squandered and wasted my life with trifles."

"Do not be so glum, my brother. I will pray for you, that happiness finds you."

"I do not think I will last that long with a heart as heavy as mine. It is hard to breathe at times. I do not sleep but pass out coughing. My eyes are heavy and burn with mucus. Ah, I long for death as I long for my lost love."

"May the Lord soothe your troubled soul," said the Pope, making the sign-of-the-cross over his brother.

Chapter 58 – A Dalliance

Giuliano was scheduled to travel to Florence, where he and his new bride would meet the King of France for his investment as Duke of Nemours, which was in north central France. In the meantime, he stayed in Rome, where he badgered Leonardo for the picture. It got so bad that Leonardo swore every time he saw him.

"Oh, Gesu Cristo!" cursed the painter. "Here comes that poor, sick Medici to beg for my painting. How many times must I tell him it is not yet finished."

"Buongiono, Maestro," said Giuliano greeting the artist at the front entrance to the Belvedere apartments where da Vinci was staying. "I was hoping I could see you today. You hinted that I might be able to visit you in your chambers and feast my eyes on that miraculous painting that you have created. I am able to give you a king's ransom for it, now that Giovanni is the Pope."

"I would prefer you give me a commission for something worthwhile," replied Leonardo. "I grow stale and bored sitting here working on mirrors all day. I cannot live on that poor stipend you provide me."

"It is all I can do at this time," answered Giuliano apologetically. "My brother controls the purse strings. You know how he favors the young pretty boys."

"Bah, Michelangelo is an ugly dwarf. I can give you pretty boys if you want."

"I want that painting, Maestro," answered Giuliano vehemently.

"As I have told you a hundred times, it is not finished," Leonardo answered just as forcefully.

"Let me see it then," pleaded the Medici. "Show me how it is not completely perfect."

"It is something that cannot be explained," da Vinci replied. "I will know it when I see it."

"You are just procrastinating. You do not want to give it up. You selfishly want it for yourself. You are in love with the damned thing!"

"See, Giuliano, you are your own worst enemy. I was going to let you view the painting, but with that outburst you have changed my mind. I value you as my most esteemed patron. You have tried your best to help me here, despite that your brother and his papal court do not value me a whit. You Medici created me, now you destroy me, but make no mistake my young friend. The painting is mine. I will determine when it is finished. In fact, it may never be finished. Only time and work will tell."

With that, the sixty-three-year-old master and his entourage went to his apartment without inviting Giuliano to join them.

As he was leaving the grounds Giuliano was accosted by a boy in livery.

"Signore," he said. "I am from a friend who would like to talk to you very much. They gave me this."

He handed Giuliano a silk handkerchief. Thinking it might be Francesco Gioconda, Lisa's husband, the silk merchant, who he knew was in Rome on business, he followed the boy. He took him to a lavish villa on top of a hill overlooking the Tiber. Giuliano waited in the vestibule curious as to who might have called him there. He supposed Lisa's husband was there to talk about the painting, but it was Lucrezia Borgia.

She swept down the stairs impetuously as if she were floating on air and didn't have a care. Her expensive gown of white satin and damask rustled with each movement. She was still attractive, with a lithe figure. Her long hair had remained golden and still reached to the ground. On closer inspection, however, Giuliano noticed winkles around the eyes and lines of worry on her forehead. She still radiated vivacity and erudition, however. She flashed a smile at him that turned sardonic when she held it too long.

"I have missed you, my dear Medici," she said. "And to think, you were right here in Rome all this time. I am here at the behest of my husband, the Duke of Ferrara. Unfortunately, he is still in Ferrara taking care of business. Or should I say fortunately?"

She smiled again, this time seductively and moved closer. She was only an arm-length away, but he had no urge to reach out to her.

"This is a surprise," replied Giuliano without mirth. "I did not expect to see you again after our last meeting. As I remember you had quite a laugh."

"I am sorry, but you were so cute, I could not help it. I have thought about that time quite often lately, especially when the Duke needs to be placated. Thinking about you and how you felt in my hands gives me great pleasure."

With that she reached down and grabbed his private parts. Shocked, Giuliano slapped her hand away and yelled out.

"Do not do that!" He was going to say more but lapsed into a fit of coughing.

"What happened to the virile man I once knew?" she said.

"He has grown old and sick with the cares of the world," he replied, finally able to speak again. "I see you still take a lot for granted."

"Should I not, after what happened that night?"

"Nothing happened. It was not my doing. You did that all on your own, if I remember correctly. I was a mere bystander. It meant nothing to me. Why have you asked me here?"

"I wanted to see you again. Is that not enough?"

"If there is nothing I can do for you, perhaps there is something you can do for me," he said.

"What? Anything, my darling," she replied in her most alluring and charming voice, her eyes laughing at him.

"There is something I want," he continued. "I would do anything if you could somehow obtain it for me."

"And what would that be?" she asked with a sly smile.

"A painting. One of the great Master's, da Vinci."

"Oh, that old charlatan. Why not get one of Michelangelo's or even better, Raphael's, who is much better looking, although I am partial to Michelangelo's male nudes. His statue in Florence, have you seen it? It is superb, beyond compare, to show a beautiful man like David so completely naked. The buttocks are better than anything I have seen in the flesh."

"And I am sure you have seen many men's asses. I see you are still bad. Do you enjoy being so dreadful?"

"It is a lot more fun than being a bore like you, who hungers for a painting," she answered. "I assume it is the portrait of your lover, that Florentine woman. Si, Giuliano, I must say you do amuse me." She laughed boisterously.

Giuliano wanted to run from the room, flee this mad witch, but he would be damned if he would run from a woman. He should have.

"I pity you, Lucrezia," he said. "You must have been awfully abused to be so bitter and mean-hearted. What did they do to you?"

"You are so smug, Giuliano. You should pity my poor brother, Cesare, who died so horribly at the hands of rebels. They stripped him naked and mutilated his beautiful body. He was only thirty-one."

She began to cry. Giuliano felt sorry for her and his old friend, but fought the feeling back. He wanted to have done with this sick, broken girl and her family.

"I do not feel pity for him or you," Giuliano replied. "Your brother was a murderer and showed no mercy for those who crossed him. You are a high-born putana. Was Cesare one of your lovers too? How many illegitimate children do you have by him?"

She struck out suddenly and slapped him before he could react, stunning him to silence.

"How many do you have, you self-righteous fool?" she said. "I will find that precious painting of yours, and when I do I will burn it."

They hurled insults and slurs at each other until two burly guards came and threw Giuliano out onto the street. He hit the pavement hard and slightly injured his hand. He felt lucky to get away with only a scratch. He had never seen a woman so angry. She actually spit at him. He wondered if she would send assassins after him.

Chapter 59 – The Last Visit

Giuliano traveled to Florence with his young bride the next day. They stayed in the Villa of Careggy. She did not travel with good grace and was without warmth. Once there, she complained about the condition of the villa and was haughty with the servants. Though Giuliano tried to sooth her with kind words, he was unable to placate her. She went to her room after supper and locked the door. The marriage was not off to a good start.

The following week King Francis I arrived in Florence to invest Giuliano as Duke of Nemours. It was a great honor, although neither he nor his spouse showed much enjoyment.

"We are in control of Naples and Milan," the king confided in him. "I will need your help ruling my Italian realms. With you, a Medici, as the king of Naples, all will be well. The people will embrace you as ruler, a son of Lorenzo the Magnificent, with my dear aunt as queen."

Philiberta fawned over her nephew, the king, and berated the household, who she did not think showed him the proper respect. Nothing was good enough for her. The fifteen-year-old from Savoy made no secret of how little she thought of Italians.

"Oh, how I wish we were in France," she lamented to the king, her nephew. "Why do we have to do this here?"

The king humored her and told her Italy was the future. It did little to change her mood.

The more Giuliano saw of his new wife, the more he missed Lisa. He imagined how it would have been if she were his wife, rather than this spoiled French brat. He thought of his child, and how happy they would have all been together, even if they were banished to the marshes of Venice. Alas, it was not to be. He had a duty to his brother, the Pope, and to his fellow Italians.

When the king went south to Rome again to meet Leo X, Philiberta went with him. Giuliano was to follow but claimed he had some business to attend to in Florence before he could go. He certainly had things to attend to, but they had little to do with the business of the city.

Giuliano had word from his brother that Francesco Giocondo was still in Rome discussing the purchase of some fine silks for the Vatican.

The news sent the younger Medici into a frenzy. It was carnival time. He sent word for Lisa to meet him at the Duomo as she had done those many years before. 'Look for the man in the white mask with a black mustache,' the message read.

The day of their rendezvous arrived. Giuliano wore a black tunic with a silver lining. Lisa wore a green, satin robe and a crimson mask that covered only her eyes. Giuliano waited by the side entrance to the Cathedral, where she had found him that night so long ago.

So much had happened since that time, so much that it seemed like centuries had passed instead of twenty years. She had married and born six children, including his little girl. He had another illegitimate son from one of his numerous liaisons. The boy stayed with his cousin, who he had been recently reconciled with after a long rift.

It was late, almost ten when she came upon him standing by the door.

"Are you waiting for someone, dear sir?" she asked.

Giuliano turned around with a smile she could not see through his somber mask.

"Why yes," he replied. "Who is it that asks?"

"I am the person you are to meet," she answered.

They threw themselves together and embraced. Taking off his mask, he kissed her passionately, unmindful of the throng of people around them.

"Ah, my love. It is you," he whispered.

"It is carnival," she replied equally excited. "I am yours for the night. Take me to our secret spot beneath the Loggia della Signoria."

A short time later they were in the Loggia, beneath the wide arch. All restraint was abandoned. They knew this was probably the last time they would be together. Both wanted to savor the other to the fullest.

"I will love you for all eternity," she told him.

"I never want to let you go now that I have you," he responded taking off her mask.

Despite how excited and happy she was to see Giuliano, she was shocked at his appearance. He looked even worse than last time. His hair was gray, his eyes deeply sunken. His complexion had turned ashen. She felt suddenly concerned but tried not to show her alarm.

"I am yours to do with as you want," she answered smiling and stroking his head.

He swept her off her feet. In spite of his weakened condition, he carried her to the bench below the archway and laid her down. To him, even at thirty-six, she was still the most stunning creature he had ever beheld. It wasn't so much her outer beauty that he saw, but her inner beauty, her gentle heart and loving nature. Compared to a bitter woman like Lucrezia or his new wife, Philiberta, Lisa was like an angel from heaven.

"You are a jewel, a treasure, a gift divine," he told her as he began to kiss the part of her costume that covered her breasts. His elegant, long-fingered hands played over her body. They were not hands of lust but hands of gentle, caressing love. It was as if he was touching her again for the first time.

"Come away with me," he begged for the hundredth time.

"It is impossible, my love," she replied. "You are married now. I have my little one to care for."

"Bring her," said Giuliano. "We can go across the sea to Dalmatia. No one can harm us there."

"The arm of the French King is long."

"It is not stronger than the Pope's."

"You would have us flee across the globe into the lands of the infidel? What kind of life would that be?"

"It would be a good life if I could be with you. Nothing else matters."

"You still sound like the boy you once were," she observed.

He was about to respond, but a coughing fit seized him, and he could not speak. It lasted for quite some time before he stopped, putting a handkerchief over his mouth. It came back wet with blood.

"My love, are you not well?" Lisa asked with concern.

"It is nothing. It will pass," he said but fell into another coughing fit.

"You must not excite yourself, Giuliano. You are not well."

"It does not matter. Nothing matters if I am with you."

"Then come, my love, take me," she pleaded. "I am yours now and forever. Love me as you will."

"No," he said, finally realizing it was hopeless. "I want you to remember me the way I was, not this decrepit shell. It is over for me."

She did not reply but held him close.

Although he wanted to make fervent love to her, all he could do was hold her with his head on her chest. That evening, while the carnival revelers danced and played above them, they laid in each other's arms, tears in their eyes. Lost in forgetfulness, they did not awake until the sun rose over the Piazza and the throngs evaporated with the morning mist. It was the last time they would see each other except in their dreams.

Chapter 60 – Perfection

Giuliano passed away in mid-March of the following year, 1516. Lisa did not hear of this until her husband mentioned it in passing a few months later. Lisa's shock was quite evident, although she tried to hide it. She stifled a scream and almost fell to the floor.

"Are you ill?" Francesco asked with alarm, giving her his arm.

She could not answer. Tears welled from her eyes. She trembled in his hands.

"It will pass," she replied. "I am surprised to hear of his passing, that is all."

"It is no mystery. He was sick with the 'white-plague'. He has led a life of debauchery. This is the result."

Lisa said nothing and tried to collect herself.

"I know you were quite fond of him once," her husband said. "But that was long ago."

"One cannot so easily dismiss the love of one's youth," she answered. "He was my first love."

What she did not say was that he was also her last.

She went to bed early that night and cried herself to sleep. Francesco did not join her until much later when she was out. She did not smile again after that, only when she saw her little girl, who was now nine, the spitting image of her mother.

With his patron now gone, Leonardo finally accepted the French king's invitation and left Italy for France. While he had not heard directly from Francis I, the king's mother, Louise de Savoie, had sent him several letters urging him to come. He was cordially received.

He and his companions were installed in the little manor of Cloux, belonging to the Queen mother. It was close to the King, who spent much of his time in the chateau of Amboise next door.

Leonardo enjoyed his new home, with its two and a half acres of gardens and meadows, a vineyard and dovecote, fishing streams and fine trees. Being free of Rome made the old master feel like a new man.

The house itself had a downstairs studio, with a spiral staircase leading to his spacious bedroom. This had a huge fireplace and large windows that looked out onto the grounds. The sixty-five-year-old artist could not have hoped for a more comfortable home to end his days.

An underground tunnel connected his house with the royal palace, so the king could visit him whenever he wanted. Given an exceptional income of 1000 ecus soleil annually, da Vinci became the king's favorite painter, engineer, and architect. Francis took great pleasure in hearing Leonardo converse about every subject under the sun. He was much valued at the French court, unlike his sojourn in Rome.

"He is the jewel in my crown," the king said to everyone.

The first thing Leonardo did was put up the painting of Lisa. Although he could no longer draw due to the paralysis in his left arm, he could still dab paint with the delicate strokes of his brush. He continued to study it, and gazed at it constantly. It remained the last thing he looked at before bed and the first thing he saw waking up.

He was captivated by the painting itself, and also by the subject. He had painted her just like he wanted, without jewels or fine clothes, in a non-traditional pose. Everything he had done, everything he had learned and experienced, all his science of anatomy, light, and color, not to mention material folds, went into the painting. This made it so natural and lifelike it seemed real. All the subtleties and art required to show motion and emotion were there. It was a masterpiece. He had created it, and he it loved it beyond all things.

The subtle smile, the lively eyes, the pearly flesh and ruby lips, the soft hair curling at the ends beneath the veil, was perfection itself. No, it was no wonder he never delivered it. He could not part with a thing so beautiful, so alive.

Her smile seemed to flicker as he stared at it, both motion and feeling intertwined, always veiled. The woman in the portrait seemed to be aware of the outside world and herself. She looked out of the painting as if seeing those who viewed her. The landscape itself showed a living, breathing, pulsing earth that flowed into her body, becoming part of it.

He realized at that moment that the painting was indeed finished. It was perfection itself. He had captured the look of love frozen for eternity in a smile.

One day shortly after he had arrived, a visitor came to see him, the secretary of a cardinal who had been traveling Italy on behalf of his master. Leonardo showed him three of his paintings – St. John the Baptist, the Virgin with Saint Anne, and a painting of a Florentine lady. All were masterpieces, but the painting that struck the cardinal's secretary the most was the portrait of the Florentine lady – Mona Lisa. He wrote back to his superior.

"All the paintings are masterpieces, but this last portrait was like none I have ever seen. She seems alive! It is as if seeing her through a window. Her eyes follow you as you move in front of her. They smile at you even as you hide her lips. You could almost imagine she is watching you as you gaze at her. It is most amazing. The Master told me it was commissioned by Giuliano de Medici."

The few years da Vinci had left went by tranquilly and happy. Then, on the second day of May, in the year 1519, Leonardo lay on his bed dying. He was surrounded by medical men and clerics. He had made out his last will and testament and had converted to Christianity. Now he was breathing his last. The King came in, distraught to see him thus, for the young monarch loved the old man much.

Lifting Leonardo's head so that he could see his face more clearly, Francis looked into the Maestro's eyes as the old man's vision dimmed. Leonardo looked like he was in a beatific trance, gazing at the pearly gates of heaven, but he was actually gazing at his painting. It was the last thing he saw. He died with a tear in his eye and a smile on his lips.

Lucrezia Borgia died that same year, after the difficult delivery of a baby boy. Many talked about her, but few mourned her. One of her last thoughts was of the Medici. She also died with a wry smile on her lips.

Chapter 61 – Love Eternal

Life went on in the Giocondo household. The children grew and left the house to seek their fortunes and marry. Francesco's prestige and influence grew along with his finances. He was confirmed as Priori of the Signoria in 1524. He and Lisa also grew closer together. He saw her as the jewel she was. She saw him as her anchor.

Francesco still lamented the fact that the picture of his beloved wife was never delivered. He learned from word of mouth that it was in the French royal palace. He told anyone who would listen that he had been the one who commissioned it, but he had given up ever acquiring it. Still, it bothered him more and more as they grew older that he did not have a picture of her in the prime of womanhood. She was still beautiful to him, even though she, too, had grown old.

In 1526 Michelangelo began to sculpt a marble statue of Lisa's lover, Giuliano de Medici, at the Medici Chapel of San Lorenzo in Florence. She went every day to watch him work until her lover's image emerged in all its glory from the stone. There he sat on his throne before her, young and beautiful and strong, dressed in Imperial Roman armor. She cried when she saw it, an old lady still lost in her dreams.

Francesco died in 1542 at seventy-seven years old of the plague that hit Florence that year. He returned Lisa's dowry to her, the farm in Poggio, still thriving after all these years. Her daughter, Marietta, who stayed with her and cared for her, took Lisa there one summer day.

They went together to the field of wildflowers, where Lisa reminisced about that stormy night. The barn where they sheltered from the rain was no longer there, but mother and daughter walked to the top of the hill where it once had been.

"I must tell you about your father before I die," said Lisa. "He was not Francesco, the one who brought you up, but a boy from my youth, who I have loved all my life and still do. His name was Giuliano de Medici."

"The one from the statue we visit in the Medici chapel?" asked Marietta

"Si, you met him one day when he came to visit us at the villa. You were eight or nine. You came out to the garden where he was sitting."

"I remember. I thought he was your father, he looked so old."

"Si, that is him. We were the same age, but he was worn down with the cares of a hard life. Ah, you should have seen him in his youth. He was so stunning, with long, curly dark hair and deep brown eyes. His hands were so beautiful, his legs so strong.

"We were in love but his father, Lorenzo the Magnificent, forbade us to see each other. He visited me here one harvest time against his family's wishes. They would have thrown us in prison if they had caught us, but he came to see me anyway, he loved me so much.

"We fell asleep together in the field here and got caught in a storm. We came to the barn that was here at the top of the hill for shelter. He built a fire, but the wolves came and threatened to eat us. Giuliano fought them off with a flaming brand. We lay naked beside the fire to dry our clothes but did nothing. We were so innocent then.

"I thought he had gone back to Florence, but the night of the harvest dance he came back in disguise and we danced together all night. Ah, what a magical evening that was.

"Then he was banished from Florence when the French came in 1495. That is the year I married Francesco. Giuliano lived in exile in Venice. It was very hard on him. He suffered greatly and grew sick. That is why he looked so old when you saw him.

"After he was exiled, I had not seen him for many years. I was sitting for the portrait I have told you about many times. It was by the great master, Leonardo da Vinci, of celebrated fame. He had come back to Florence after several years absence, to finish the painting. Unbeknown to everybody, including Francesco, Giuliano came back with him. He showed himself to me while the master was painting me. I ran to him as I did in the field of flowers and we made love. That is how you came about, and why I have loved you so among all my children. You are his."

"I thought you loved Papa, I mean Francesco. I always thought…"

"I did love Francesco, very much. He was a wonderful, gentle, thoughtful man, and was in many ways a true father to you. In a way, you have two fathers, the one who brought you into the world, and the one who brought you up. You were born out of love and nurtured in love. But the love I had for them is different. Francesco I respected and admired. He was so good to me, and I will always honor his name and be grateful for his kindness and generosity. Giuliano was my first love and my greatest love. I thank God for that gift, that I was granted that kind of passionate love."

Her daughter looked at her mother differently from that day forward. The Medici statue took on a whole new significance for her.

A few years later, Lisa became sick, and Marietta could no longer care for her. She took her mother to the Convent of Della Stufa, where she lived for several years, cared for by the sisters, until she passed away in 1551 at the age of seventy.

As Lisa confessed her sins to the priest, she slipped into a coma, a dream world, where she was talking to Giuliano again, as if he was still there.

"Oh, my love, I am so grateful, for I have had the most wonderful life. I've been so blessed to know a love like ours. It grew from a child's love to that of a woman's. Though we could not live together as man and wife, our love grew to surpass all bounds. I have loved you all my life. All my days were filled with love for you. I know that you loved me also, that even though you could not live without me, you went on living and loving me anyway. I do not know many things, but one thing I am sure of. Our love is eternal. I will never stop loving you even in death."

With that Mona Lisa breathed her last breath and died with a shy smile on her lips and a tear in her eye.

Fini

Author's Note

This book was inspired by a chapter in Serge Bramly's book, 'Leonardo – Discovering the Life of Leonardo DaVinci'. It talks about the lack of information on the chronology of many of the Master's most famous paintings, including the Mona Lisa. However, new scholarship has apparently uncovered many of these age-long secrets about the painting.

His wonderful book not only tells when the painting was worked on, but who commissioned it. There are numerous anecdotes and traditions regarding the painting and the person as well. For instance, Vasari, Leonardo's early biographer, writes that it was commissioned by Lisa's husband, Francesco Giocondo, a wealthy silk merchant in Florence, Italy. Another tradition indicates that Giuliano di Medici commissioned it. Their families were connected and they may have known each other as children. Some say they were lovers.

No date is given for when the painting was done, although recent evidence indicates 1503 being the likely date, when Lisa was twenty-four. She would have been married for almost ten years by this time, and had several children.

The painting was never delivered, although it was obviously completed, for no painting could ever look more perfect. There is no evidence that any commission was ever paid. The fact that Leonardo had it with him when he died, also adds to the mystery of the painting. But what about the mysterious smile? This book tells what might have been, a wonderful story just waiting to be told.

I have made extensive use of this chapter of Bramly's book for my descriptions of the painting itself and for research on Leonardo's and Lisa's lives. I hope you enjoyed reading it as much as I enjoyed writing it.

ALSO BY JOSEPH W. BEBO

Lake, Land, and Liberty

Family Legends – The Charbonneau Letter

Lamp of the Gods

Bach Again

In the Back of the Van

Stricken: Quantum of Revenge

The Shivering

My Terrible Mistress

The Shot

Altered Realities

Alex – A Lesson in Courage

Waiting to Take Off

The Lawless Chronicles (Almost Dangerous, Sometimes Deadly, and Forever Fearless)

Siege et Survie

Dancing on the Moon – A Romance